No Groom at the Inn

No Groom
at the Inn

A Dukes Behaving Badly Novella

Megan Frampton

AVONIMPULSE
An Imprint of HarperCollinsPublishers

Excerpt from *One-Eyed Dukes Are Wild* © 2015 by Megan Frampton.
Excerpt from *Montana Hearts: Her Weekend Wrangler* copyright © 2015 by Darlene Panzera.
Excerpt from *I Need a Hero* copyright © 2015 by Codi Gary.
Excerpt from *Blue Blooded* copyright © 2015 by Shelly Bell.
Excerpt from *Best Worst Mistake* copyright © 2015 by Lia Riley.

EPub Edition November 2015 ISBN: 9780062412980
Print Edition ISBN: 9780062412997

10 9 8 7 6 5 4 3 2

No Groom at the Inn

Agamist:

1. A person opposed to the institution of matrimony.
2. A thick fog specific to bodies of fresh water.
3. A compound of iron and salt.

CHAPTER ONE

1844
A coaching inn
One lady, no chickens

"Poultry."

Sophronia gazed down into her glass of ale and repeated the word, even though she was only talking to herself. "Poultry."

It didn't sound any better the second time she said it, either.

The letter from her cousin had detailed all of the delights waiting for her when she arrived—taking care of her cousin's six children (his wife had died, perhaps of exhaustion), overseeing the various village celebrations including, her cousin informed her with no little enthusiasm, the annual Tribute to the Hay, which was apparently the highlight of the year, and taking care of the chickens.

All twenty-seven of them.

Not to mention she would be arriving just before Christmas, which meant gifts and merriment and conviviality. Those weren't bad things, of course, it was just that celebrating the season was likely the last thing she wanted to do.

Well, perhaps after taking care of the chickens.

The holidays used to be one of her favorite times of year—she and her father both loved playing holiday games, especially ones like Charades or Dictionary.

Even though he was the word expert in the family, eventually she had been able to fool him with her Dictionary definitions, and there was nothing so wonderful as seeing his dumbstruck expression when she revealed that, no, he had not guessed the correct definition.

He was always so proud of her for that, for being able to keep up with him and his linguistic interests.

And now nobody would care that she was inordinately clever at making up definitions for words she'd never heard of.

She gave herself a mental shake, since she'd promised not to become maudlin. Especially at this time of the year.

She glanced around the barroom she was sitting in, taking note of the other occupants. Like the inn itself, they were plain but tidy. As she was, as well, even if her clothing had started out, many years ago, as grander than theirs.

She unfolded the often-read letter, suppressing a sigh at her cousin's crabbed handwriting. Not that handwriting was indicative of a person's character—that would be their words—but the combination of her cousin's script and the way he assumed she would be delighted to perform all the tasks he was graciously setting before her—that was enough to make her dread the next phase of her life. Which would last until—well, that she didn't know.

Sophronia was grateful, she was, for being offered a place to live, and she didn't want to seem churlish. It was just that she had never imagined that the care and feeding of poultry—not to mention six children—would be her fate.

She hadn't been raised to think too highly of herself, an impoverished earl's daughter couldn't, no matter her bloodlines. But she'd thought her father had put by enough money to see her through to find a cottage somewhere, somewhere to live with her books, and her wit, and her faithful maid, after he'd left this mortal coil. But while her father had been very specific when it came to ordering which text of ancient Greek poems would suit his needs the best, he had been less so when it came time to providing for his daughter's future after his eventual, and inevitable, demise.

He'd left her with practically nothing, in fact.

Hence the chickens.

Which was why she had spent a few precious pennies on a last glass of ale at the coaching inn where she was waiting for the mail coach to arrive and take her to the far reaches of beyond. A last moment of being by herself, being Lady Sophronia, not Sophy the Chicken Lady.

The one without a feather to fly with.

Chuckling at her own wit, she picked her glass up and gave a toast to the as yet imaginary chickens, thinking about how she'd always imagined her life would turn out.

There were no members of the avian community at all in her rosy vision of the future.

Not that she was certain what her rosy vision of the future

would include, but she was fairly certain it did not have fowl of any kind.

She shook her head at her own foolishness, knowing she was giving in to self-pity by bemoaning her lot. It was more than many women had, even ladies of her station. She might have to take care of children and chickens—hopefully in that order—but she would have a roof over her head, food to eat, and clothing to wear. Perhaps the holiday season would be one of celebration. Celebrating a roof over her head, for one thing.

"All aboard to Chester," a voice boomed through the room. Immediately there were the bustling sounds of people getting up, gathering their things, saying their last goodbyes.

Sophronia didn't have anyone to say goodbye to. Her maid, Maria, had found another position, even though she'd wept and clung to Sophronia until the very last minute. But Sophronia's cousin had made it very clear the invitation was for one lady in distressed circumstances—namely, Sophronia—and there was no room nor salary for a lady's maid.

So she drained her ale and stood, rising up on her tiptoes for one last stretch. As tall as she was, it was difficult for her to retain any kind of comfort in a crowded coach for any period of time, and she knew the journey would be a long one.

That she would be cramped and uncomfortable for longer than the actual coach journey was a truth she was finding very hard to ignore.

"Excuse me, miss," a gentleman said in her ear. She jumped, so lost in her own foolish (fowlish?) thoughts that she hadn't even noticed him approaching her.

She turned and looked at him, blinking at his splendor. He was tall, taller than she, even, which was a rarity among gentlemen. He was handsome in a dashing rosy-visioned way that made her question just what her imagination was thinking if it had never inserted him—or someone who looked like him—into her dreams.

He had unruly dark brown hair, longer than most gentlemen wore. The ends curled up as though even his hair was irrepressible. His eyes were blue, and even in the dark gloom, she could see they practically twinkled.

As though he and she shared a secret, a lovely, wonderful, delightful secret.

Never mind that all those words were very similar to one another. Her word-specific father would reprimand her, if that gentle soul could reprimand someone, that is, and if he heard how cavalierly she was tossing out adjectives that all meant nearly the same thing.

But he wasn't here, was he, which was why she was here, and now she was about to find out why this other he was here.

Far too many pronouns. Her attention returned to the tall, charming stranger.

Who was talking to her. Waiting for her response, actually, since she had spent a minute or so contemplating his general magnificence. And words, and her father, and whatever other non-chickened thoughts had blessedly crossed her mind.

"Can I help you, sir?" Sophronia asked. He was probably lost on his way to the Handsome Hotel where they only allowed Exceedingly Handsome guests.

That he might think she'd know where the Handsome Hotel was gave her pause. Because she was not handsome, not at all.

But what he said next was even more unexpected than being asked to provide directions to some establishment where one's appearance was the only requirement for entry.

"Would you marry me?" he said in a normal tone of voice, as though he hadn't just upended Sophronia's entire world.

Cachinnator:

1. One who cashes in on an opportunity.
2. A loud or immoderate laugher.
3. The element of a spinning wheel that feeds the wool
   through.

CHAPTER TWO

"It will be two weeks. At most, three." His mother beamed at him, as though the prospect of a house party in the country during the holiday season with people he did not know was some sort of rare treat.

It most definitely was not.

Jamie began to walk around the room, unable to stay seated for longer than a few minutes, at least when he was at his mother's house. Which usually made him regret being so generous to her, since she had most of the things he'd sent her on display, which made walking around even harder. "And who will be in attendance?" There had to be a reason she was so insistent he accompany her. It wasn't just that she didn't get to see him enough; he knew that look in her eye. The one that said, "I've got plans for Jamie, and they are probably going to bring him very little joy." Not that she thought that, of course. She only thought about what she thought he might like, and he always felt like the worst kind of ungrateful wretch when it turned out he did not like what she'd presented, whether it was a special meal, or a new watch, or a house party when he'd rather just stay in London, when everyone else was gone.

He'd gotten very good at pretending to be pleased when that was not what he was at all. But that was better than watching her face fall in disappointment.

He'd seen how his father hadn't been able to pretend, how it ate away at him. How he compromised what he truly wanted in order to keep someone else happy. Jamie was determined not to let that happen to him.

She shrugged, as though it wasn't important. Which only meant that it absolutely was. "The Martons, the Viscount Waxford and his family, and Mrs. Loring and her daughter. Oh, plus the hosts, of course. The Greens are the loveliest people."

"And how many of them have unmarried daughters?"

She shifted in her seat.

Jamie stopped pacing to look at his mother. "That many, hm?"

She couldn't seem to quite meet his eyes. "Well, I have heard that Lady Marigold Waxford is a beauty. All golden curls and bright blue eyes. The Greens' daughter is apparently quite studious, she is usually away at school, but has returned home for the holidays. She has quite a tidy fortune, and is said to be a good conversationalist. And the other two, well yes, they have daughters who are friends with the Green girl."

Jamie swallowed through a suddenly thick throat. "Four young ladies, then?" Could just the thought of four young women at a house party make a person choke to death?

It felt like that, even though he desperately hoped not.

But his mother wasn't paying attention to how difficult it

was for him to breathe, nor could she know how her words seemed to wrap themselves around his neck. "You never know, James, when you might find someone you like. When are you going to settle down?"

Jamie opened his mouth to reply, but snapped it shut as he thought about her question. *When are you going to settle down, Jamie?*

It was a question she had been asking, off and on, since the first time he had left England to go on one of his "funny trips," as she called them.

That his funny trips were as necessary to him as breathing wasn't something they discussed. He'd tried to, once, but she'd merely grabbed her handkerchief and sobbed quietly into it as he told her how he felt as though he might explode if he stayed in one place too long.

He had seen the same thing play out when he was a child, when his father tried to change the way things were. It just wasn't done. Which was why Jamie had to do it.

It wasn't as though he didn't love his mother; he did. And it wasn't as though he needed the money that his funny trips brought. His father had left him more than enough money, even if all the elder Mr. Archer had done was sit on a sofa and drink wine. No, Jamie lived for the adventure of it, the finding of a treasure that was hidden in plain sight, something that only he could discern. He was doing the thing his father, he thought, had always wanted to do himself. Finding treasures.

Jamie always brought the treasure back to England and sold it to someone who craved adventure as much as he did, but had to be content with experiencing it through objects, not actual living. He rarely kept a treasure, not for himself.

If Jamie ever stopped, he thought he might die.

And yet—and yet sometimes, when he was lying awake at night in another place that wasn't England, he wondered if it was enough.

Of course it is, his mind would go on to assert.

But his heart begged to differ.

"Actually, Mother, I have something to tell you," he began, knowing he was making possibly the stupidest decision he'd ever made—and that included the purchase of something he'd thought was an ancient papyrus that turned out to be a creative child's way of demonstrating how annoying she thought her parents were—but unable to stop himself once he'd started. "I am betrothed."

For once, his mother had nothing to say.

As soon as the proposal left his mouth, Jamie had the urge to punch himself in the face.

Judging by the expression on the lady's face, she felt the same way.

At least they were in agreement.

He closed his eyes and grimaced. "That wasn't exactly what I meant," he said, letting out a deep breath as he spoke.

"So you're saying you don't wish to marry me?" At least she wasn't screaming or hitting him. That was something.

"No, I mean, yes, I mean—" He gestured at the chair she'd just risen from. "Could we sit down and discuss this?"

She glanced over his shoulder, a concerned look knitting her brows together. "I am supposed to get on the mail coach, the one leaving in a few minutes."

"This will take only a few minutes to explain," Jamie replied, hoping to God it was true.

She tilted her head and gave him a look of appraisal, then nodded her head. "Very well. Only a minute, mind you. I can't be late for the chickens."

Jamie opened his mouth to ask about that, but snapped it shut again as she sat. He didn't have time to ask questions about what she might possibly mean, not when his future as an unencumbered bachelor was at stake.

He sat down, as well, scooting his chair forward so he could speak quietly to her. *Speaking in a low voice will not make this any less outrageous*, a voice in his head reminded him.

But it could perhaps persuade her that he was not actually insane. Or remarkably presumptuous.

"The thing is," he said, speaking both quickly and quietly, "I am in need of a fiancée, but just for a short time." Judging by the expression on her face, he was not doing any better at explaining himself. "The thing is," he said again, wishing he could just snatch her up and present her to his mother without having to bother about explanations and such, "I might have just told my mother I am engaged to be married."

"And you are not." It seemed she understood a bit of it, at least.

"No. Nor do I wish to be."

"Despite what you just asked me." Now she sounded amused, and he allowed himself to feel a little hope that she would understand him, at least, even if he failed to convince her to help him.

He had to admit he hadn't planned on asking a random stranger to marry him—few people did—but when he'd burst out of his mother's house, having told her he was engaged, of all things, he'd known that a drink was in order, and he also knew where the nearest place to obtain said drink was.

And then he'd strode in, desperate and thirsty, and had seen her. A slender woman sitting by herself, looking off in the distance like some wise goddess, Athena or Minerva or whatever she was called, a simple traveling bag at her feet, a worn cloak wrapped around her against the cold.

She was entirely alone. Alone and traveling during one of the coldest months of the year, close to the holidays when families got together. Only he didn't think she was going to her family—her expression would have been expectant, not resigned. Unless she had an unpleasant family, in which case perhaps she would be just as happy to leave with him as on the mail coach.

He liked to think he was a better choice than an unpleasant family, especially given what he had to offer her.

"My mother is here, living in London, only she's taken it in her head to go to a house party in the country, and there are many unattached young ladies there. And, and you haven't met my mother—"

"I haven't even met you," she interrupted in a tart tone.

"Right, well, Mr. James Archer at your service." He held his hand out and she regarded it with one arched eyebrow, as though contemplating what he might do if she allowed him to take her hand.

It honestly hadn't occurred to him to do anything, but now that she had that eyebrow raised, and her manner seemed to waver between entertained and aghast, he wondered just what she'd do if he took her hand and walked her out of the inn.

Probably scream. So that was not a good idea.

Thankfully, she did allow him to grasp her hand for a brief handshake. "I am Lady Sophronia Bettesford," she replied. She spoke in a measured way, as though every word was held up for examination before being released from her lips.

"It is a pleasure to make your acquaintance, Lady Sophronia." Jamie tried to summon up his most charming smile, but even with his ingenuity with women, he was at a loss when confronted with this situation—how did one behave toward a woman one might have deliberately not proposed to?

"And yours, Mr. Archer." She glanced to the door, where people were lining up to board the coach, presumably. "But I do have to be on that coach, and while I appreciate the opportunity not to marry you, I cannot take any more time."

She had a title—he hadn't anticipated that; he'd just seen she was Quality. She was well-spoken, she seemed to take things in stride, and she was relatively attractive.

He was not going to find a better potential bride-not-to-be anywhere.

"What would it take for you to do this? It would last a month, at most, and then you could get on your coach and go to wherever you are planning to go." He heard the desperation in his voice, and hoped it would sway her toward him, rather than making her want to run away.

She knitted her brow and stared at him, so intently he had the feeling she could see inside to his soul. Hopefully she'd see how much he wanted his mother to be happy, not any of the things he knew might make him seem to be a bad person—his ability to talk a potential seller into letting go of that treasure for a lower price than the seller had asked for, his equal ability to persuade women to give up their treasures in bed, his need to be on the go, constantly.

His selfish wish to live the life he wanted even though it might—it did—hurt his mother.

"I would want enough to purchase a cottage somewhere. I have no idea what that would cost, and it is likely far more than you'd want to pay for a pretend betrothed," she said, lifting her chin as though in defiance. As though now he was the one who might run away screaming. "And I would want your assurance that this is all the time you would require of me, that you wouldn't need me to return and pretend to be your wife or anything later on." She took a deep breath. "If you can give me those things, I will do this for you."

"Last call to Chester!"

They both glanced to the door, to where the stable boy was calling.

"Well?" she asked, reaching down to her valise.

"Done," he said. His happiness and his mother's happiness—in opposition to one another—were worth whatever he'd have to pay.

"Then we have a bargain, Mr. Archer," she replied, raising her hand from the valise's handle and holding it out to him.

"A bargain," he repeated, shaking her hand.

Otosis:

1. A skin affliction that causes discoloration.
2. Mishearing; alteration of words caused by an erroneous apprehension of the sound.
3. Remaining in a state of suspension.

CHAPTER THREE

"Your purchasing clothing for me is not part of our bargain," Sophronia said as she walked hurriedly after Mr. Archer—her new betrothed.

He turned to look at her, a roguish smile on his lips. He had a remarkably lovely mouth for someone who appeared so otherwise masculine. Not that lovely mouths weren't masculine, but she had never actually noticed a gentleman's mouth before.

Now it seemed that was all she could think of. Well, that and that he was determined to buy clothing for her, when she was perfectly capable of buying her own.

Except she really wasn't. She hadn't even tried to get her money back for the coach. She knew that would be a fruitless endeavor, and what with the ale she'd bought and the rest of the money she'd carefully secured away so she could eat on the journey—she might have had enough for one sleeve.

And, her new betrothed told her, they were on their way to a house party. One where getting appropriately dressed was one of the ladies' primary activities.

So while she could object, she knew he was right. She just didn't want to make him spend more than he already had to—she was fairly certain that fake betrotheds, if there was a market price for them, cost far less than what she had demanded.

Who was to say he wouldn't find another, less expensive betrothed somewhere?

But meanwhile, as soon as they'd shaken hands, he'd taken her from the inn and began walking, very quickly, toward a place he assured her would have gowns suitable for her, and that could be made in time so they could make the journey the day after next.

"Excuse me, Mr. Archer?" she ventured, wondering how he could walk so fast without it seeming to be a strain. Likely something to do with his long legs.

And now here she was thinking about his legs, and the long strength of them, in addition to his mouth.

Perhaps by the time their month together was complete she would have inventoried his entire self.

Although that was not something she should be contemplating.

"If we are to persuade people as to our relationship, Lady Sophronia, you should call me James. Or Jamie, that is what my mother calls me," he said, flinging the words over his shoulder without losing his speed. "And I will call you— Sophy? My lamb? Sophycakes?"

"Sophronia will do just fine," Sophronia replied, as stiffly as she could manage given that she wanted to laugh— Sophycakes?

"Sophronia is not nearly as much fun," he returned.

He had a point.

"But what did you want to ask, Sophronia?" She didn't have to see his face to know he was smiling—he spoke as though they were both in on the joke, whatever the joke was.

She hadn't felt as though she'd been included in anything even close to a joke for a long time. It felt—lovely. Nice. Wonderful.

Again, she heard her father chastising her for saying basically the same thing three different times, but "lovely" was sufficiently different from "nice" and "wonderful," wasn't it? And now she felt all three.

"I don't have a place to stay this evening. If you know of a respectable hotel," *and can pay my bill*, "I can stay there this evening, and then join you on the journey to"—and she didn't even know where they were going—"to the house party."

He stopped and spun around to face her, so abruptly it made her gasp. But then again, that could be because she was struck, again, by just how handsome he was. Would anyone believe he had chosen her? It wasn't that she thought ill of herself—she didn't—but she did know that while nobody would bat an eye at his taking up residence in the Handsome Hotel, they would likely quibble if she were to attempt to book a room at the female equivalent—the Pulchritudinous Pub, for example, or perhaps the Ideal Inn.

Somewhere, she heard her father cheering her expansive language.

"You can stay at my house," he began, only to hold his hands out to her as he saw her reaction. "That is, at my mother's house. I am staying there as well, but she will be a more than suitable chaperone. Besides," he added, his mouth quirking up in a rueful smile, "she will have many questions to ask you." He frowned, as though struck by something. "We need to get you a lady's maid, however. Mother will know something is awry if you just appear alone."

Sophronia's heart leapt. Of course, she would be able to be reunited with Maria, who was spending her last night of freedom at her sister's house in Cheapside. "I have a lady's maid I can obtain, that is no worry at all."

"Good, good," he said distractedly. "You can send a note to retrieve her while you are being fitted at Madame Fairfax's establishment. And then we can return to my mother's house, and I can introduce you. We will need to better acquaint ourselves with one another so as to make our story plausible."

The enormity of what she—what they—were doing struck Sophronia so sharply she gasped again, and this time it was not in appreciation of his pulchritude.

"It will be fine, you will see." It was as if he had read her mind, even though not a moment ago it had seemed he had been thinking of something else entirely.

"Yes, I just—" She paused, then blurted it all out. "I just want to be certain you will not regret this, we don't even know how much it will cost for a cottage, and then there's the expense of the clothing, and my maid, and the travel, and—" She heard her words roll faster and faster, and her heart sped up in rhythm.

"Breathe, Sophronia," he replied, taking her hands in his. She gazed down at his fingers, noting how large they were, but still shapely, sprinkled with hair on the back of his hand.

She had moved on from his mouth and legs, it seemed. She heard herself laugh, a breathy, nearly hysterical laugh, and felt the rush of what this could mean for her—for her whole future.

She couldn't ruin this, either for him or for herself. The rest of her life depended on it.

Taking a deep breath, she lifted her head and looked into his eyes. "I am breathing, James," she said in a measured tone. Close-ish to the way she normally spoke, at least. "Thank you for the kind offer," she said, feeling her mouth curl up in a half smile. "I promise you, I will do my best to be the betrothed you require."

He lifted her hand to his mouth and kissed it, keeping his gaze on her face. "We are in this together, Sophronia. I promise you in return, I will uphold my end of the bargain and will also do my best to be the betrothed you are worthy of."

Her throat got thick at hearing the obvious sincerity in his voice. And then she wondered if she was getting into even more than what she'd expected.

Jamie took his betrothed's arm—Sophronia, not Sophycakes or even just plain Sophy—as they walked up the stairs to his mother's house. They'd spent two hours at the dressmaker's shop, and thankfully Madame Fairfax had exercised discretion, not commenting on how this young lady was so markedly different in looks and style than the other ladies Jamie had brought to her shop before.

He glanced over at her as they waited for the door to be opened. She was remarkably tall, so tall he would guess her to be only five or so inches shorter than he. It was refreshing not to have to bow his head down to look at her. And he found he did want to look at her—something in her face, something in her dark brown eyes, in her expression, made him want to discover who she was, why she was in that coaching inn, what made her needs so modest that a remote cottage would suit her.

He hadn't been in London or among Society so much as to have the breadth of English aristocracy at his command, so he had no idea who her father the earl had been, or where she had lived before arriving at the inn. He knew, however, that she was a lady, in more than just the titled sense; there was something so elegant about her, her movements, her way of speaking, that was both appealing and off-putting. As though she were a beautiful diamond who would cut you if you got too close.

Jamie should remind himself of that, he thought—not to get too close. She wasn't at all like any of the women he'd found intriguing before, but for some reason, she intrigued him.

"Ah, Mr. James," his mother's butler said, a welcoming smile on his face. Taylor had been with his mother for years and treated Jamie as someone to be tolerated for her sake. Jamie knew the warmth of Taylor's smile was in direct correlation to how many times his mother must have sent Taylor outside to see if her son had returned yet.

He was surprised there wasn't a path on the carpet in the hallway indicating the poor man's footsteps.

"Yes, we are back. If you could inform my mother—"

"You're back!"

"Never mind, Taylor, I see she is here." Jamie took a deep breath before turning to face his mother. This was it. He had to persuade her that not only was he betrothed, but that he was deeply in love with his bride-to-be. He knew Sophronia's favorite color was green, she preferred novels to poetry, she liked ale, and she had a way of pausing before she spoke that made him think she was truly considering her words.

He hoped his mother would keep her questions to those important topics so they wouldn't be found out.

"Allow me to introduce my betrothed," he said, drawing Sophronia forward. Her hand trembled. "Mother, this is Lady Sophronia Bettesford. Sophronia, this is my mother, Mrs. Archer."

She withdrew her hand from his arm and held it out to his mother, who gaped at it, then stepped forward and gathered Sophronia into a hug, which meant the much taller woman had to stoop to be embraced. "I am so delighted to meet you, my dear. Jamie kept you such a secret, I didn't even know he was acquainted with any lady who might be worthy of him, much less you!" She released Sophronia but kept hold of her arms, gazing up at her with an expression something close to rapture. "You are so lovely, I am certain we will be as close as though I was your own mother," she said, her words coming out in a sob.

Sophronia darted a startled look at Jamie, but her expression was serene when she looked back at his mother. "I am delighted to meet you as well, Mrs. Archer. This was all rather unexpected," she said, in such a dry tone Jamie nearly choked on his laugh, "so it is not surprising to hear this is the first time you have heard of me."

"Come into the sitting room, dear, and let me hear all about you."

His mother took Sophronia's arm and led her into the

room, chattering nonstop about her general delight at Jamie having brought her home. "Even though an indication that this was happening would have been nice," she said, with a sharp look directed at Jamie. He followed them, feeling some of the knot of tension in his chest untie, just a bit, that the first encounter seemed to be going well.

Now they just had to get through the next two, perhaps three, weeks without anyone realizing they'd met only earlier in the day, and that neither one of them had any intention of marrying the other.

Jamie had once successfully negotiated the purchase of artifacts that were reportedly the only things keeping the town from being destroyed by angry gods, so he thought he could handle the relatively minor endeavor of persuading his mother and the guests at a house party that he was, indeed, engaged to be married.

Even though he rather wished he were back facing those superstitious villagers rather than attempting this subterfuge.

Vecordy:

1. Senseless, foolish.
2. A harmonious sound.
3. The change of seasons.

CHAPTER FOUR

"**M**y lady!" Maria shrieked as she was shown into Sophronia's bedroom. She'd been given the best bedroom, according to her new not-yet mother-in-law, and Sophronia had to admit it was substantially better than the place she'd lived in most recently, when she'd still held out hope that something could keep her from her cousin, and his chickens.

And now, just when she had given up and was resolutely headed to become an unpaid chicken-and-children herder, he'd appeared.

"Maria, how lovely to see you, and isn't this incredible?"

Maria hugged her, and Sophronia felt immediately better—she had spent only a day or so on her own, without any kind of human discourse (beyond the purchasing of the coach tickets, not to mention the ale), and she hadn't realized just how bereft she had felt without anyone to connect to. Until Maria wrapped her in an embrace.

"Now, now, my lady, why are you crying?" Maria sounded perturbed, as she should—Sophronia never cried, not even when she'd come to the conclusion that her father had, indeed, left nothing for her. "Why are you here? Is there anything I can do?"

Sophronia drew back from her friend's embrace and shook her head. "I am fine, this is really an amazing story, I just—I think I am just overwhelmed."

Maria nodded toward the bed. "Let's just sit down and you'll tell me all about it. I have to say, you could have knocked me over with a feather when the note arrived, telling me to come here posthaste."

Thankfully I will not be knocked over by any kind of feather, not if I do this properly, Sophronia thought to herself. It seemed she could leave the chickens behind, but they would not leave her.

"So you just have to pretend to be engaged to the gentleman?" Maria said after Sophronia had related the details. Put that way, it did sound rather easy.

"Yes, and I have to persuade his mother that I am a suitable bride for her son, which is the most important element." The lady was so sweet, and obviously adored her son. Already Sophronia felt bad about her part of the deception, at fooling the woman who only wanted her son to settle down and have a family. A fact she had repeated no fewer than a half dozen times while they were having tea and getting "better acquainted."

If all the people she was to meet in the ruse were as talkative as Mrs. Archer, there would be no concern about having the lie discovered—she had barely gotten a word in edgewise, and the words were limited to "yes, please" and "just milk."

"You will do fine. And then—and then you'll have enough for us to go to the country?" Maria's tone was hopeful and wistful; they'd talked about what they wished they could do when they knew there was no chance of it. That Maria was still hesitant about the possibility made Sophronia's heart hurt, even as she was thrilled their dream could become reality.

And then what? a voice asked in her head. *You buy a cottage, you and your maid go to live there, and then what? You spend the rest of your life alone?*

She had to admit the voice had a point. She hadn't thought much past leaving London and being able to survive without having to become a poor relation. What if that was all there was to her life? Things that were less bad than something else?

Was that a way to live? Now it was her father's voice talking to her, and she frowned. It was because of his daydreams, his refusal to settle for less than the best, to look to the future, that she had been landed here in the first place. He didn't have a say in what she was going to do for the rest of her life, given how he hadn't thought of it at all while he was alive.

She would just have to adopt her father's viewpoint, ironic though that felt; she would get to the point where she was in the cottage, but wouldn't think beyond that.

"Yes, we'll be able to go to the country, and buy a little cottage, and live there. Forever." Even to her own ears, she didn't sound delighted at the prospect, but thankfully Maria was focusing on the words, not how she said them.

"Thank you, my lady," Maria said in a fervent tone. "We will persuade all of them. We have to."

And that was the truth of it, wasn't it? "Yes, we will."

Sophronia walked to the wardrobe in the corner of the room, opening the doors to reveal a few gowns that Madame Fairfax happened to have on hand. The rest she'd promised for the following day. Sophronia hated to think of what the workers would have to do to make that happen, but she needed the clothing in order to make this work, so she couldn't spare sympathy for a tired dressmaker. Hopefully the women there would be compensated. She'd tell her betrothed of her concern, perhaps ask him to send them some of what he had promised to give her. "And here are some of my disguises, so you can help me dress for dinner."

Maria followed her, her hand reaching in to touch the gowns with a near palpable reverence. "Oh, my goodness, these are lovely. Not only will we get our cottage, you'll have these gorgeous gowns, as well."

"And no chickens to waste them on," Sophronia muttered under her breath.

Jamie wasn't prepared for the sight he saw as Sophronia walked down the stairs for dinner. He'd known she was tall, and slender, but beyond that, he hadn't noticed much except her suitability for the task.

But now, dressed in one of Madame Fairfax's gowns, she was a different word than "beautiful"—she was glorious. The amber sheen of the silk brought out the gold highlights in her brown hair, and made her brown eyes glint gold, as well. The gown was simply adorned, something Madame Fairfax had insisted on, since Sophronia was so tall, and any kind of furbelow would make her look awkward.

Jamie had to admit that Madame was correct. Sophronia looked like she was a goddess in truth, descended from Mount Olympus to take pity on mere mortals by blessing them with her presence. Her figure was flattered by the cut of the gown, the soft swell of her breasts showing above the fabric, the center dipping down in a V that made him want to see what was underneath.

Her waist was tiny, and then the gown flared out below, no doubt hiding long, lissome legs. She met his gaze, a hesitant look in her eyes, and he felt his chest tighten that she didn't know, that she didn't enter the room knowing what she looked like, and the effect she was having on him.

But given that this was an entirely fake betrothal, perhaps it was good that she didn't realize any of it. He was intrigued, of course, but he most definitely did not want to become entangled—that was the whole purpose of this deception, to keep his way of life and make his mother happy.

Although the thought did cross his mind that they were technically betrothed, after all, so he might have to do some of the things one did with one's betrothed.

If one were quite, quite intrigued.

And not determined to leave the country at the earliest possible moment.

"You look lovely, Sophronia," he said, taking her hand in his and raising her fingers to his mouth. Her eyes widened as his lips made contact with her skin, and he wondered for a moment what she would do, how she would react, if he were to turn her hand over and press a kiss into her palm.

And then immediately vowed to himself he absolutely should not satisfy his curiosity. It would not be fair, either to her or to himself, to mix that possibility into their business agreement.

They were to be intimately acquainted for less than a month, and then they would leave one another, him to travel, knowing his mother was pleased, and her to her cottage, wherever that might be.

"Let us go in to dinner. Mother is waiting," he said, retaining her hand in his and leading her to the dining room.

"Just one moment, please." She sounded shaky, and he had to wonder if she was having second thoughts.

"I don't—I just wanted to say thank you for this." She uttered a little snort. "Thank you for the opportunity to pretend to be someone I am not so I can avoid having to deal with poultry for the rest of my life."

That explained the chickens—somewhat. "You are welcome," he said.

"Only," she asked, "what will you tell your mother later on? I won't be in London when this is over. How will you explain that?"

"Easy," he said smoothly. "I will make some excuse about why we have to get married elsewhere, then we will leave to do just that, and then when I return, you will be staying there, taking care of our numerous children."

She blanched. "Numerous—?"

He exhaled. "Well, that part probably isn't wise. Mother will wish to see her grandchildren. I might have to kill you off, I hope you don't mind."

Her eyebrows rose up, her eyes wide. "Kill me off? How are you going to do that?"

He waved his hand in the air. "An inconvenient snake, a

village uprising. Don't be concerned, you will be far away by the time you die."

"Good to know," she replied drily.

He hadn't quite worked out all the details, honestly, but he had to deal with the situation one step at a time. Or, rather, one false betrothal at a time. He knew well enough he could persuade his mother of anything; she had believed him when he'd told her he had developed a sudden, but not fatal, illness that could only be cured by eating an entire apple pie. He'd been five at the time. He hadn't eaten apple pie since.

"Now, let us go persuade my mother we are hopelessly in love."

He held his arm out for her, and she looped her arm through his, fitting perfectly to his side.

Her skirts rustled as they walked into the dining room, and Jamie detected a faint floral scent—he couldn't identify which flower, just that it wasn't overpowering and he found he liked it more than he might have originally thought.

Or was that just her?

Laetificate:

1. To make joyful, cheer, revive.
2. A portrait done in miniature.
3. The lower level of a raised garden.

CHAPTER FIVE

"Allow me to present my son's intended, Lady Sophronia Bettesford." Mrs. Archer spoke to an older woman with a faintly disapproving air. That was probably due to Mr. Archer having arrived with a betrothed in tow. Given what he'd said about the available ladies, and his desire to escape them.

Sophronia dipped into a curtsey, feeling her muscles protest at the movement. Six hours in the coach with Mr. Archer and his mother had resulted in her feeling like she'd been wrapped around herself and tied into a few knots—she couldn't imagine how Mr. Archer felt, given that he was so much taller. He stood next to her, not showing any sign of travel strain. But then again, perhaps that was because he traveled so frequently—his mother had spent nearly an hour listing, to comic effect, the various countries her son had been to in the course of his work, something Sophronia vaguely understood to be the buying of things from one place to sell to people from another.

She had to pretend to cough when Mrs. Archer announced her son had been in Paws Hill when she meant

Brazil, and then couldn't stifle her laughter at her saying Jamie had found the most wonderful cotton in Eyesore—meaning Myosore.

Thankfully, the lady herself was well aware of how she muddled things, and laughed the longest and loudest when her son gently corrected her.

"Sophronia, this is our host, Mrs. Green, and her daughter, Miss—?"

The disapproving woman drew a younger version of herself forward. "Miss Mary Green."

"How do you do, Mrs. Green, Miss Green?"

"And you hadn't met my son yet, had you? Of course when I first accepted your kind invitation to spend the holidays together, I had no idea we would be bringing his future bride! I do so appreciate your making room for dear Sophronia. She is the best Christmas present." The Green ladies' expressions indicated that, indeed, they were not quite so pleased as Mrs. Archer at this development.

"Thank you for the invitation, Mrs. Green." Sophronia kept her voice as pleasant as she could, given the looks in the other ladies' eyes.

Mrs. Green looked as though she were about to sniff in disdain, but merely said, through a pursed mouth, "You are welcome, Lady Sophronia." She regarded all three of her newly arrived guests as though they were things to be allocated somewhere, not people to interact with. Sophronia hoped Mrs. Green's guests were not as severe as their hostess, or she would be longing for the chickens.

Or forced to spend hours with Mr. Archer.

She darted a glance over at him, wishing that her pretend betrothed wasn't quite so impossibly good-looking. And charming. And intelligent. And patient with his somewhat scatter-brained mother.

She let out an involuntary sigh, and felt his elbow touch her arm. "Are you all right?" he whispered, as his mother was engaged in a long description of the carriage ride to the house, which was apparently far more interesting than Sophronia had experienced.

"Yes, I am fine," she replied softly. *And observant*, she would have to add in her assessment. Her father had often told her he could see what she was thinking, she was that easy to read, and she would have to guard her expressions here, among all these strangers. And Mr. Archer.

Who was no stranger, not now, not when she'd seen the amused smirk on his face as he recited the list of possible nicknames. Or seen his expression as she'd descended the staircase in her new gown, the one that made her feel like a princess, not a lady who was down on her luck and (hopefully) would not have to pluck. Or cluck.

And now she was allowing her mind to wander, to practically gallop through the forest of her imagination, where she was witty, and not alone, and had a future that wasn't one that just featured her and her maid off in a small house somewhere.

That was dangerous, especially since a distinctly tall, handsome, and observant gentleman was lurking nearby in her imagination as well, now doing whatever it was he would do after looking at her like that.

She shivered, just thinking about it.

"Lady Sophronia is chilly," Mr. Archer announced, taking

her arm. "Perhaps you could take her up to her room, and she could lie down before dinner?"

"I'm not—" Sophronia began, only to snap her mouth shut as she realized she was about to contradict him, her betrothed, and she didn't want anyone—particularly the Green-Eyed Monster ladies—to think there was any kind of discord between them. "Ah, yes, thank you, that would be lovely," she said in a stronger tone.

"You will meet the rest of the party at dinner," Mrs. Green said, waving her hand over her head to summon the housekeeper who'd apparently been waiting in the shadows. "The Martons have had to cancel"—a swift glance to Sophronia revealed why—"but the Viscount Waxford and his family will be here later on. Dinner is at eight o'clock. We keep country hours, you see."

"This way, my lady," the housekeeper said.

"Rest well, my dear," Mrs. Archer called as Sophronia began to walk up the stairs. "And do you know, Jamie met his bride-to-be at an exhibition of Arty Facts?" Sophronia heard her pretend future mother-in-law say.

"Artifacts, Mother," Jamie replied. She wished she had been down there to see his expression at his mother's colorful language.

Three hours later, Sophronia was wearing the most lovely gown she'd ever seen in her entire life, Maria had outdone herself with her coiffure, and yet she knew she was the most despised person in the room.

"My lady," the Viscountess Waxford asked, leaning past

the vicar, who'd arrived to round out the table, Mrs. Green explained, with yet another look toward Sophronia, "how did you meet Mr. Archer?"

Her words asked how they had met, but her tone implied, "how did you dare?" A young lady with light blond hair and the most enormous blue eyes sat two seats down from the viscountess, and also appeared to want the answer to the question. Perhaps the viscountess's daughter? Goodness, there were certainly an enormous number of unwed girls here. No wonder James had been so desperate.

Mr. Archer answered before she had the chance to. "My beloved Sophy and I first found a commonality of spirit in our shared love of hieroglyphics."

Sophronia blinked, realizing she wasn't quite certain what hieroglyphics were. Or was. She didn't even know if they were singular or plural.

But no matter, nobody was questioning the veracity of Mr. Archer—James's—words. Not when he was sitting at the table, all tall, charming, roguish self of him, his entire manner setting out to charm, to persuade, to convince, to deceive.

For goodness' sake, she nearly believed his words, and she knew full well they hadn't met because of hieroglyphics. And she hoped she wouldn't be asked to repeat the word, because she was imagining she would mangle it as thoroughly as Mrs. Archer would.

"What are your favorite ones, Mr. Archer?" Miss Green asked. She was apparently studious, judging from what her mother said. She blinked myopically in the candlelight, her youth and petite self and protective mother all making Sophronia stupidly, ridiculously jealous. And too tall.

Or that could be because of the way Mr. Archer was looking at her. As though she was the only woman in the world he wished to gaze upon. Sophronia hated herself for wondering if Miss Green could even see it, since he was across the table.

And then wondered what she would do, how she would feel, if he were to look at her like that.

She felt suddenly hot and restless, as though there was a heat storm about to roll through her general vicinity. Not that she knew what a heat storm was as much as she didn't know what hieroglyphics were, but that was how she felt.

"I find it so hard to choose, Miss Green," James replied. He shot a quick glance toward Sophronia with an accompanying curl of his lips.

Yes, the same lips she couldn't seem to get her mind off of. And somewhere her father was yelling at her about ending a sentence with a preposition, not the fact that she could not stop thinking about a man's mouth.

Father's priorities were always off.

"I think I like whichever one my Sophy likes," he continued. Sophronia had to concentrate not to let her mouth drop open. What was he doing? Was he trying to reveal the falsehood? Could he just not help himself? Or was he being so clever at trying to make it appear that they were truly and well-acquainted that no one would question them?

Which was a lot of words that basically meant, "I am not certain what hieroglyphics are, much less which ones are my favorite, and I don't know why he had to possibly expose the reality of our situation to all these people who are at this moment wondering who I think I am."

Instead of saying any of that, however, she pretended for

a moment she was him, and thought of what he might say in reply. She glanced toward him and gave him as warm a smile as she could manage, given that she wanted to strangle him. "My favorites are the ones you showed me when we first met," Sophronia replied, imbuing her tone with as much honey-cloying sweetness as she could.

His answering grin, the spark of recognition in his blue eyes, caused that heat storm to flare up into something almost tangible—as though he were touching her, running his fingers down her neck, onto her spine, making her tingle everywhere.

All of that didn't mean she wasn't still aggravated with him, and worse, for jeopardizing their subterfuge, but it did mean that she wished she could find out what his mouth felt like. Firsthand. Or firstlips, so to speak.

All of the other ladies in the room, even the married ones, appeared to feel the effects of his charm. Mrs. Green had shed some of her haughty demeanor to ask his opinion on the epergne in the middle of the table, while the viscountess had told him she was interested in finding candlesticks that would suit her Oriental sitting room, keeping her hand on his sleeve as she described in exact detail what the room looked like.

Meanwhile, Mrs. Archer just observed, smiling widely, seeming blissfully unaware of all the currents of want flowing through the room—the ladies wanting Jamie, Jamie wanting (apparently) to irk Sophronia, Sophronia finding she wished to discover a way to disturb his casual charm.

"My lady, you are the Earl of Lunsford's daughter, are you not?" It was the vicar—Mr. Chandler, she thought—addressing her, thankfully taking her attention away from the current conversation between James and the girl who was indeed the viscountess's daughter, who seemed to believe she had been an African princess in a previous life.

"Yes, I am. That is, I was. Father passed away two years ago." Leaving behind a massive amount of books, little debt, but even fewer funds for his daughter.

"I am so sorry, my lady. I was a great admirer of your father's, I might even go so far as to say we were acquaintances. He and I exchanged a few letters on etymological issues several years ago. I keep those letters still."

"Ah," Sophronia replied. "Father was an avid correspondent." He rarely left the house, in fact, preferring to live his life through books and letters rather than venturing outside. In hindsight, perhaps it was just as well; if he had gone out more, he would have spent more money, and Sophronia would have been among the chickens much earlier than this. There definitely would not have been the opportunity Mr. Archer had presented.

"Do you share his love of words?"

Sophronia opened her mouth to respond in the negative, but realized that wasn't the case. "I do," she said, feeling a fragment of warmth at the memory of her father. She'd lost her mother too young for her to recall, so it had been just her and him for as long as she had awareness. "Father made the very startling decision not to hire a governess for me, so he oversaw my instruction. He was an engaging teacher, even if his skills at maths left something to be desired." That went a long way toward explaining his financial difficulties. She didn't know if he was even aware of just how dire their straits were. Although he would know for certain that it was "straits," not "straights."

"You were so lucky to have the benefit of a mind like that," the vicar said in an admiring tone of voice.

"I suppose so," Sophronia replied with a smile, unable to deny his enthusiasm.

"Would you—do you suppose you would be so gracious as to visit my rectory and see some of the books I've collected? I know your father approved of some of my purchases, he was very helpful in advising me about them." He seemed to realize what he'd asked her, and turned a bright shade of red. "That is, with your betrothed, of course, and perhaps others of the party who would like to visit."

Sophronia suppressed a giggle at Mr. Archer being forced to go look at someone's musty collection of books when, from what she had gathered, he was a collector of remarkable and often dangerous artifacts, nothing nearly so prosaic as books. Written in English, no less. "We would love to, Mr. Chandler, thank you for the invitation."

It would serve him right for the whole hieroglyphics incident.

Wheeple:

1. The handled end of a sword.
2. Melancholy; prone to sadness.
3. To utter a somewhat protracted shrill cry, like the curlew or plover; also, to whistle feebly.

CHAPTER SIX

His pretend betrothed was ending up being far more bothersome to his state of mind than he would like, Jamie thought sourly. He glanced down the table to where she was in an animated conversation with a youngish gentleman that Jamie thought might be the curate, or one of the young ladies' brothers. He was gazing at her with what looked like near adoration.

And Jamie couldn't blame him. Just as she had the previous evening, Sophronia was wearing a lovely gown that seemed as though it had been specifically designed to make her look as beautiful and goddesslike as possible.

Its lines were simple, in stark contrast to the gowns the other women were wearing—this gown had one frill trailing from her waist diagonally to the other side, ending up at the bottom, serving to highlight just how tall and willowy she was. The bodice was simple as well, fitted perfectly to her frame, showcasing the slope of her elegant shoulders and the strength of her slim arms.

But the color was what made it hers. The gown appeared

to be either brown or purple, the colors shifting depending on how she moved and where the light caught the fabric. It was daring, unusual, and distinctive—like, he was coming to understand, his fake betrothed herself.

And he did not like the way the young man was looking at her, still. He wanted to be the one gazing into her dark brown eyes, the recipient of her quick, shy smile.

More than that, however, he wanted to hold her in his arms and find out what it would be like to kiss a lady who was nearly his height.

It was purely the jealousy of a male who was accustomed to being the center of female attention, he assured himself. While also feeling like a spoiled child.

But no matter why he felt the way he did, he knew one thing—the gift he wanted most for this holiday season was a kiss from her. Despite what he'd vowed before. A kiss, just one kiss, couldn't do any harm, could it? And if it brought joy to both of them—holiday joy, the joy of the season, and he knew it would bring joy to her, he had been told often enough of his kissing prowess—then it would make the season brighter.

One gift, that was not so wrong to wish for, was it?

And he was going to do his damnedest to get it.

"Sophy," he said, striding toward her as the men returned to the drawing room where the ladies sat, drinking their tea after dinner.

He'd met the man who'd so engrossed her during dinner. The vicar, who apparently had known Sophronia's father and chattered on about some sort of book collection he had that she had agreed they would both go see. Not a threat, then.

She looked up at him, arching her eyebrow in a faintly dismissive manner, which only served to make him want to fluster her even more. "Yes, James?"

Good. She was addressing him by his first name now. He smirked at the thought of suggesting she call him by a nickname—"lord and master," perhaps, or "future perfection." He knew that would irk her as much as it would amuse him.

"Mrs. Green was telling me about some of the items she's collected, and she wanted me to take a look at them. I was wondering if you would like to accompany us?"

"My daughter is just as knowledgeable about the collection as I am, Mr. Archer," Mrs. Green said, raising her voice as she spoke over the distance between them. "Lady Sophronia has just gotten a fresh cup of tea, we wouldn't want to disturb her."

Jamie met Sophronia's eyes, and he saw perfect understanding there. Thank goodness.

She placed her teacup on the table next to her, then rose in one elegant movement. It looked like water flowing upstream, or a tree nymph emerging from her woodland home.

Or a tall, lovely woman standing. When had he ever been poetic like that before? He'd have to say never. Not that backwards-running water sounded like anything Wordsworth or any of his cohorts would say, but it was definitely more colorful than he had ever been before.

"I would love to see your collection, Mrs. Green, thank you so much for thinking of James and his interests in these things. I share his interest, that is but one of the things we have in common." She walked to where he stood and took his arm, gazing up at him with an adoring glance.

Bravo, he wished he could say, only that would totally give the game away, wouldn't it?

"My son has always been interested in old things," his mother said. From the spiteful glint in Mrs. Green's eye as she heard the comment, Jamie knew the woman was thinking of Sophronia's age, and he wished he could deliver some sort of cutting response.

But they were spending at least two more weeks here, and he wouldn't do anything to disturb his mother's pleasure, even if it meant enduring looks and comments for the entire time they were there.

Plus it would just mean he would find more reasons to escape to be alone with his betrothed, and perhaps he'd get his Christmas present early.

"James, a word, please." It was the end of the evening—the very long evening—and Sophronia was exhausted, as much from being on her guard as from having traveled all day.

He, she thought grumpily, looked as fresh and handsome as he had that morning when they'd gotten into the coach. His charming smile remained in effect, hours into the excruciating evening, although perhaps it wasn't quite as excruciating for him as it had been for her. Or a different kind of excruciating; he was wanted by nearly all the ladies in the general area, whereas she . . . was not.

She'd dutifully accompanied him to view what appeared

to be some old, dingy pieces of tin, the "collection" of which Mrs. Green was so proud. Mr. Green seemed to not have an opinion about anything whatsoever, merely nodding in reply to any question posed him and devoting all of his interest to his dinner and later, his brandy.

Miss Green refused to be daunted by Sophronia's presence, clinging to James's arm as they walked the hallway to the room where the collection was kept, Sophronia trailing along behind like a tall afterthought.

Until James paused and waited for her to come alongside him, then took her arm on his other side so the three of them were walking abreast. Sophronia couldn't help but be touched by that courtesy, even though it also proclaimed his marital intentions, and thus served his purpose in bringing her along in the first place.

"What is it, my dear?" He grinned at her, as though fully aware just how his epithet would make her feel, and delighted by the prospect of her reaction—whether annoyance or amusement, she wasn't sure. A mingling of both, likely as not.

"Could we step outside for a moment?"

His grin got deeper. "You are aware, are you not, that it is December? And therefore likely to be quite cold?" He glanced around at the rest of the company. "Unless you know I can keep you warm."

"Jamie!" his mother exclaimed. "You'll embarrass Sophronia!"

And Mrs. Archer was right. Although now her cheeks felt as though they were burning, and heat was spreading through her body so she knew she would not be cold outside at all.

So he had managed to keep her warm after all.

His eyes were laughing as he took her arm and guided her toward the door to the hallway. "We'll be just a moment, not long enough to cause a scandal," he called as they walked.

"Do you enjoy doing that?" she asked exasperatedly, then answered her own question. "Of course you do, or you wouldn't do it."

"Do what?"

They reached the door, at which a surprised footman waited. "Yes, we're going outside just for a moment," James said.

"Can I fetch the lady's wrap?" the footman asked.

"I won't need it," Sophronia replied, still feeling as though she were burning from the inside out.

"Excellent, my lady," the footman replied, unable to keep the dubious tone from his voice.

The night was cold, but not frigid, and it felt entirely refreshing after being in the stifling—in all ways—atmosphere of the drawing room.

They stood on the stairs, a light showing from the stables to the right of them, the moon casting a glow over the driveway and the gardens in the distance.

It was so blessedly and wonderfully quiet. It seemed he appreciated that as well, since he didn't speak, just kept hold of her arm as he guided her down the stairs, across the driveway and just up to the gardens, which had a light dusting of snow.

Sophronia hadn't seen snow in its natural state perhaps ever—her father rarely wanted to go to the country, and even when he did go, it was in the fall or spring. A snow in London quickly turned to slush, the only remnants of the real thing lingering on the trees for a day or two after. Until that, inevitably, melted to join the slush on the streets and the sidewalks.

"What did you want to speak to me about?" His voice was quiet, as though he was reluctant to break the silence.

"I don't even know." Well, she did, but she didn't want to ruin the stillness. "Or I do, but it seems so silly, given what we're doing."

"Let me guess—the hieroglyphics?" His words sounded amused again. What must it be like to walk around continually amused? She wished she knew. Then again, if she did know, she would likely be insane, and she did not wish for that.

"Yes. That. You could have warned me."

"And missed the look of surprise and outrage on your face? You are very expressive, Sophy."

"Sophronia," she corrected.

He leaned into her, and she felt the warmth of him, his solid shape at her side. It would be so easy to lean into him as well, to take this moment for what it was, to relish, perhaps the only instance—depending on what her future held—to spend time and flirt with a handsome gentleman who was just what he said he was.

Which was a man entirely determined to remain unencumbered by a woman, who was so desperate to avoid said entanglements that he would go so far as to fake a betrothal, to run the risk of having his much beloved mother find out that he was lying, in outrageous fashion, to her.

To be known as the kind of man who would do such a thing in order to avoid walking down the aisle.

So perhaps she would not lean back.

"It is my turn to thank you," he said, startling her.

"Why?" *Because I have just vowed to stay immune to your charms? Good luck with that, Sophronia,* she thought to herself.

"Because if you were not here, if I was forced to face this situation on my own, it would be far more dreadful, even without adding in the possibility that I would find myself engaged to a woman I did not want at the end of the holiday." He paused as Sophronia was parsing out what he was saying. "That is likely why I chanced discovery." He shrugged, as though embarrassed. "It isn't something I seem to be able to help. If there is a worse thing than being stagnant, than being immobilized by one's life circumstances, I don't know it."

"Hence the traveling," Sophronia replied. She was starting to feel the cold, and felt herself shiver.

"Here." He must have felt it, too, which wouldn't be surprising, given their arms were touching and she could almost swear she felt his hand hovering somewhere behind her, not quite on her body but not quite not on it, either. "You can wear my jacket. I just wish to stay out here a little longer." He removed his jacket before she could protest, then draped it around her shoulders, tucking it in at her waist with a frown of concentration drawing his eyebrows together.

The jacket was warm from his body, and was redolent of his scent, a mix of soap and something that smelled spicy and faintly exotic.

Of course, faintly exotic to Sophronia was anywhere outside London, so perhaps his cologne or whatever it was came from York or Devon or something.

"I don't know when it first began, but I just remember

having to sit still while being given some lesson or another, and feeling as though I wanted to burst out of my skin." He stared up at the sky, his breath showing visibly in the cold air. "My father used to talk about how much he wished he could just escape, but he had us, and my mother is not a good traveler." He shrugged, as though it didn't matter, when Sophronia could tell it absolutely did. "I don't think it's fair to ask someone to live a life they don't want to live." His voice sounded almost lost. As though it was the young Jamie speaking, not the adult one standing beside her. "If I could move all the time, I think I would. Unfortunately," he said with a laugh, his tone audibly changing, "there are such essential things as sleep, and visiting with one's mother."

"You love her very much, don't you?" Even in his jacket, she was shivering, but she didn't want to go back in, not when she had the chance to speak with him out in the open—in so many ways.

"I do. I would do anything to keep her happy." He paused, then continued. "Anything, that is, except marry someone when I'm not ready to."

They were both silent for a time, each looking up at the sky. The one place, Sophronia mused, that he hadn't been yet.

"My father and I were on our own, much as you describe with your mother." They did have things in common, Sophronia realized. Just not hieroglyphics. "It often felt to me as though it were us against the world." She shook her head, burrowing herself further into his jacket. "Not that we were against anything, but we were on our own. Just us."

"You have no other family?" he asked, a surprisingly soft tone in his voice.

She thought of her cousin, and her cousin's children, and the chickens. "Not precisely. I do, but none I wish to be with. That is why I was so willing to take you up on your offer. Or non-offer," she said with a laugh.

He didn't reply. He seemed content to be still here, just standing beside her, his head flung back, the strong lines of his throat showing fierce and strong.

Add throat to the list of body parts she was now thinking about.

"We should go in, you're freezing," he said after a bit. He took her arm without waiting for her reply—something characteristic of him, she was coming to realize—and walked her back into the house, her mind jumbled up with cold, and Christmas, and what home meant, and why someone would find it impossible to stay in one place, even though that one place held people who loved him.

Gyrovague:

1. Loss of freedoms.
2. One of those monks who were in the habit of wandering from monastery to monastery.
3. The outside circle of a compass.

CHAPTER SEVEN

"Today we thought the young people in the company would take the carriages and visit the abbey. It remains as it was when Henry II reigned, and I am certain Mr. Archer and my own dear girl will find plenty to admire." Mrs. Green issued her words like a proclamation, leaving no possibility of declining. "As well as the rest of the party," she added, even though it sounded as if "the rest of the party" was an afterthought to Mr. Archer and her own dear girl.

Sophronia looked to where Mr. Archer—James—sat at the breakfast table, a bleary look on his face as though he were still sleeping. Perhaps he did not like the mornings as she did—she found she did her best thinking at that time, much to her night-owl father's chagrin.

She felt her lips curve into a smile as she recalled just how many times he wanted to discuss some new discovery he'd made after a long evening of reading, only to get exasperated because she was so tired.

"Something amusing, my dear?" He was so observant,

even when looking as though he were still lying in bed, the covers tangled about his—

Oh, no. Now she was thinking about his torso. Who knew the study of anatomy was so fascinating to her?

"Nothing in particular, my dear," she replied, stressing the last two words. He grinned back at her, his eyes lighting up with a shared amusement.

He was altogether too charming, even when half-asleep. Especially when half-asleep.

"The visit to the abbey sounds delightful, Mrs. Green," Jamie said, turning to speak to their hostess. "My Sophy was just saying the other day that she hadn't visited enough ancient abbeys in her lifetime." He spoke without a hint of amusement in his voice, as though he were entirely serious.

How did he do that? Sophronia had to bite her lip to keep from giggling, and meanwhile, he had an entirely serious mien.

And yet—and yet when she met his gaze he winked at her, which just made her want to laugh and smack him at the same time.

Or do something else entirely.

Oh, dear. She had known him for no more than a few days, and she was already entranced by his charm. Not really a surprise, given how charming in general he was. But dangerous—her father had been equally charming, albeit in an entirely different way, and she couldn't trust charm like that. What was it hiding? The inability to plan ahead? A need to do what one wanted—read books or travel to exotic lands—rather than taking care of one's responsibilities?

Rather than choose to live a compromised life?

Fine. She could admire him, even find him charming, but

she could not trust him. In the time she'd known him, he'd come up with an elaborate ruse to avoid matrimony, risked discovery by teasing her, and nearly made her give herself away through laughter.

Although she could admire him, as she'd said, and she most definitely did that. She hadn't known before that a gentleman's appearance could have such a—*visceral* effect on her, even though that was likely entirely the wrong word.

Sorry, Father.

Disturbing. Enchanting. *Beguiling.* He was fascinating, and she teased herself now with the thought that perhaps it would not be so bad to allow herself some harmless fun and flirtation while she was inhabiting this disguise.

It would be entirely expected, would it not? After all, a distant betrothed would be seen as even less of an impediment to a marriage-minded miss (or her mother) than one who was constantly hanging around her beloved.

So she would constantly hang around him, if only to satisfy their bargain, and to ensure he wasn't trapped by someone else while they were here.

It would be a lovely Christmas present to give herself, something she hadn't even known she wanted, but now she knew about it, it was all she could think about.

Thus settled, Sophronia listened as Mrs. Green laid out the very exact details of their day.

Mornings, Jamie invariably found, came far too early. Especially when one's hostess insisted on speaking very stridently before one had had one's full complement of coffee.

He'd discovered the beverage while traveling in Turkey, and while English people didn't make the drink with as much ferocity as the Turks did, he found it essential to his ability to remain awake during the first few hours of the day.

"Did you sleep well, Jamie?" His mother patted his hand as she spoke, and he covered it with his own in an almost unconscious gesture. It had always been this way—her worrying about him even though she usually had no resources to solve what might have been bothering him, and often exacerbating the problem.

Such as arranging his presence at a house party with a veritable cricket team's worth of eligible young ladies. His gaze darted to his betrothed, looking alert and untroubled at the other side of the breakfast table, her entire self exuding a quiet composure that settled him, somehow. Quieted his restless spirit.

She truly was lovely. He didn't think he would call her beautiful, necessarily, and "pretty" was far too mundane a word for how she glowed. She was striking, like a lush tree standing by itself in the middle of a green field. At the moment, all of her attention appeared to be on her breakfast, her gaze lowered to the plate in front of her, so he could look at her as much as he liked.

And he found he liked to. The viscountess's daughter, seated beside her, was pretty, definitely, but her looks seemed immature and insignificant when compared with Sophronia's. Even Mrs. Green's pleasant—and intelligent enough—daughter seemed less by comparison.

Sophronia, his betrothed, was a woman, a strong, smart, capable woman. One who quaffed ale in a public house as easily as she did tea in a gentleman's breakfast room. One who spoke of her childhood with a quiet solemnity, who found a way to soothe him through their common experience.

That was far more alluring than the most beautiful girl.

He was very much looking forward to his self-prescribed Christmas gift, and he hoped it wouldn't take him too long to receive it.

"I slept well enough, Mother," Jamie replied at last. It was only while sleeping, actually, he found he could remain still for longer than a few moments.

Being unconscious would do that to a person.

"Mrs. Green, may I compliment you on the softness of your pillows?" Jamie said, taking the last swallow of coffee and gesturing to the footman to refill his cup. "I have slept in some remarkably unpleasant places, and it is a treat to sleep in a proper English bed." He paused, then something entirely wicked within him made him add, "I only wish I'd had someone with whom to revel in the comfort."

Sophronia had just taken a bite of something, but choked at his words, a whoosh of crumbs flying up from her plate as she coughed. She raised her head and glared at him, as much as saying, "how dare you," and he wanted to laugh aloud.

It was entirely too much fun to irk her, to watch the pink flow into her cheeks as he ruffled her feathers.

"I order the bedding from a fine establishment in London," Mrs. Green replied, apparently ignoring both Jamie's words and the fact that her guest was choking on one of her breakfast offerings. "I do find that English goods are so much better than foreign ones, don't you?"

Mrs. Green, Jamie decided at that moment, was an actively obnoxious person. It was as though she were setting out to be deliberately unpleasant. Or at the very least, exceedingly protective of her own country's goods. "Mrs. Green, I am not certain I can agree with you," Jamie replied. "After all, my vocation is the purchasing of items outside of England that British people are desirous of." He spread his hands. "If I did not believe that things outside of our fine country were valuable, I would be wasting my own time, wouldn't I?"

Mrs. Green's mouth pursed, and her expression faltered, as though she was warring within herself to argue with him because she didn't agree with him, or allow the point to pass, because she still had hopes for her daughter, regardless of Sophronia's presence.

She chose the latter course, and he had to say at least she was stubborn, as well. "Perhaps, Mr. Archer, that is so."

Jamie glanced over at Sophronia, who had gotten her breathing under control, and met her gaze, feeling the reassuring warmth of her understanding practically radiating out from her.

There was something so addictive about that comfort, something he'd never experienced in another person's presence in his entire life.

With certain objects, yes—there was a carved statue of some ancient god or another he'd found while in Africa, and he'd kept the statue for longer than he normally would because of how he felt when he looked at it.

He had felt it almost like a tangible loss when he'd finally let it go, but he didn't want to be encumbered by anything— not an object, or a person, or anything that could tie him down, make him stay still for longer than a few moments.

Or two to three weeks, depending on the circumstances.

It felt as though he had the statue back in his possession, in fact, because of the way he felt when he looked at her. Knowing she understood, at least partially, some of what he was going through, what he was enduring in this enforced holiday.

Speaking of which, at least he was being given opportunities to explore, to move, to see things that would engage his interest.

Well, things that were in addition to the thing—the person—most engaging his interest, his pretend betrothed. Whom he didn't have to pretend to find entirely engaging.

Queem:

1. The first bud of a flower; more generally, the first indication of Spring; behold, the queem of Spring.
2. Pleasure, satisfaction. Chiefly in *to (a person's) queem*: so as to be satisfactory; to a person's liking or satisfaction. *To take to queem*: to accept.
3. To consider oneself higher than another; conscious of one's position in life.

CHAPTER EIGHT

"I didn't expect this." James spoke in a different tone of voice than any Sophronia had heard before; he sounded almost reverent as he gazed around the small chapel in the abbey.

He had insisted she sit beside him in the carriage, and she'd been acutely conscious of his body—those legs she couldn't seem to stop thinking about—just next to hers, his large hands clasped on his knees, the scent of him seeming to seep into her skin.

Miss Green and the viscountess's daughter also joined them, sitting opposite. When not guided by her mother, Miss Green was a very pleasant conversationalist, if shy. The viscountess's daughter was much more talkative, and most of her talk revolved around what people thought of her—namely, that she was the most lovely girl in the room at any moment.

Sophronia spent a few joyful moments pondering what it would be like if Mrs. Archer and the viscountess's daughter were left alone in a room together, neither showing much ability to listen to another person.

But that was mean to Mrs. Archer, who was likely just

lonely. It sounded as though James was away far more often than he was here, and it was clear her life revolved around her son, and the vast amount of concern and love she had for him.

Sophronia promised herself she would spend some more time with Mrs. Archer. That is, before the holiday was over and James killed her off in some horrific way.

Wouldn't that be more upsetting to Mrs. Archer than to have him just tell her he did not wish to be married?

Although telling her would be to confront his problem head-on, and she had the feeling he was unaccustomed to that, being far more used to using his vast amount of charm to wriggle out of a situation.

Like her father. Another reminder to keep her guard up.

"Look, here," James said, startling her out of her thoughts. He had taken her hand and was leading her to a dark corner of the chapel. A table was placed there, several items gleaming dully in the darkness on its surface.

He paused before the table and dropped her hand, reaching out to lift up one of the items. A large vessel, it appeared to be, with whorled edges and a wide lip.

"What is that?" Sophronia asked, interested in spite of herself. There was something so contagious in his manner, in how he held the vessel with a near reverence but still caressed its curves.

Sophronia felt her eyes roll at herself as the imagery made her think of things she should absolutely not be thinking of, in a chapel, no less.

"It is a pitcher," he said in a less reverent voice.

Sophronia uttered a snort, surprised by the mundane

plainness of his words. "So nothing special? A goblet for holy wine or an offering of flowers to pagan gods or something?"

"I didn't say that," he replied, setting the pitcher back on the table. His movement was graceful and cautious, revealing his attitude toward the pitcher and whatever it might be. "It was used by the people who worshipped here. To serve their water, or wine, or whatever they were drinking, during celebrations." He turned to look at her, his eyes riveting in his handsome face. "Just imagine what it was like to be here, all that faith and love and family in one room. Maybe they were honoring a fallen family member, or celebrating a successful harvest or something. Like when we celebrate the holidays. And they'd be sharing the feelings and also sharing something to drink, something to sustain them. Something to bond them in this time of togetherness."

She felt shaky as she met his gaze. "That is—that is amazing," she said, speaking of how he'd described things, the moment in this room a few hundred years ago, rather than the pitcher itself. "No wonder you are so successful in your work."

He smiled, but it was a rueful smile, one tempered by some sort of—loss? Longing? "I used to wish I could have lived back in those times, where one remained in one place for one's entire life. Not to have the opportunity to travel, unless it was to wage war, and I certainly did not wish to do that. To be constrained by circumstances rather than open to opportunity."

She stepped forward and touched his arm. "Why?"

He shook his head, not meeting her gaze, looking at the ground. "It seems I've always wished to belong somewhere, even though I chafe against it." He raised his head and looked into her eyes. She felt the force of that blue stare all the way through to her feet. He was charming, and unreliable, and was even now telling her he would never settle down, never live up to his responsibilities.

And yet she wanted to savor him in this moment, in these few weeks they had together during their pretense.

She stepped forward again, not even knowing what she was planning, only fairly certain of what she was about to do.

"Lady Sophronia," Miss Green called from the back of the chapel, "and Mr. Archer, do come look at this marvelous triptych." And just like that, the moment was gone, and whatever she'd thought about doing was swept away by the duty of going to view a triptych, which sounded nearly as indecipherable as whatever hieroglyphics were.

But the fragment of the emotion she'd felt radiating from him—that feeling of wanting something, of yearning, remained, and she was left with the desire to help him. Or if she were to be entirely honest with herself, she was left with the desire for him. She recognized the inherent loneliness in him—she had it herself—and she knew, with even more resolution, that it wouldn't do any harm for them to assuage their loneliness together, if only for a few weeks.

That, more than mild flirtation or even a stolen kiss or two, would be her gift to him. He deserved it, especially since soon enough he would be rid of her and back to his nomadic ways.

Jamie cursed Miss Green's interest, at least at that very moment. He had gotten good at discerning when a lady was about to do something less than circumspect, and he'd seen the determination in Sophy's eyes as she regarded him. The determination and the desire, along with perhaps a spark of mischief.

That definitely intrigued him. He wouldn't have said, upon first meeting her, that she had a mischievous spark. She had too much of her goddess mien on display, which of course made sense since when they first met he'd proposed. Falsely.

But now that he'd spent some time in her company, he'd glimpsed things about her he wondered if she even knew about herself—that she had a sense of humor, that she was capable of deception, but even more, that she was an understanding soul, someone who seemed to sympathize with his situation, though he knew full well he could be derided for it—after all, what relatively young man wouldn't want to be the focus of female attention, especially when the females were all just as young, comely, and had their respective attractions? If it weren't him in the situation, he would mock the man who bemoaned that particular fate.

But not her. She'd gauged the situation and offered acceptance, and assistance, and even, he thought, a sense of commonality, though he had no idea what her own difficult position was.

Except that of course there must be one, or else he wouldn't have found her in a coaching inn drinking ale on her way . . . somewhere, with no family and no objection, after the usual reasonable ones, to embarking on this charade with him.

He wanted to know more about her, about why she had family, but had decided not to be with them, but had instead taken a great leap of faith in agreeing to their bargain; but he was also keenly aware that the more he knew, the more entangled he would become. He couldn't afford entanglements, at least not emotionally. He could afford them literally, which was why he was willing to give her so much for just a few weeks of her time.

But the cost of an emotional entanglement—that was far more than he was willing to pay. Which made her understanding and sympathy even more dangerous to his piece of mind.

But meanwhile, he couldn't resist the urge to find out more about her. To give in to the pull he felt to be with her, to see what it would be like to kiss a goddess.

He would just have to stay on his guard, which he'd been doing his whole life.

"What have you found, then, Miss Green?" he asked, following Sophy as she headed toward the back of the chapel. He'd found a treasure, he thought, and not just the pitcher on the table—a treasure he could keep for just a bit, just long enough to soak in its warmth, and feel the calming stillness, if only for a moment.

Peragrate:

1. A half-measure.
2. To travel or pass through (a country, stage, etc.).
3. The closure to a teapot.

CHAPTER NINE

"And after dinner, we will play games, as we always do during the holidays." Again, Mrs. Green didn't make a suggestion so much as issue a command.

Sophronia wondered if the woman would take it amiss if she saluted in response.

And then wanted to laugh, because of course she would.

They'd spent another hour at the abbey, Jamie walking around the place with great strides and gazing at each of the objects in the gallery for far longer than Sophronia would have deemed possible.

For a man who claimed to be so restless, he was definitely able to be still when he was engrossed in something.

Sophronia shifted in her chair as the ramifications of that thought crossed her mind. She couldn't seem to help it, she immediately looked his way, something she had done for most of the dinner. She'd barely concentrated on the food, actually, since her mind was swimming with images of him, his expression as he looked at yet another ancient dusty object, how intent he seemed.

There was something so moving about it, and yes, something so intriguing, as though she weren't already intrigued.

(She was entirely intrigued.)

What would she do if he were to turn that attention, that specific, engaged attention to her?

He had somewhat already, but it was nothing like the way he had looked as he'd stalked around, picking something up and just holding it in his hand—that large, strong hand, *for goodness' sake, Sophronia, think of something else*—regarding it with a keen interest that sent shivers down her spine.

What could she do to incite and engage his interest? Why was she even thinking about it?

Well, that last one she could answer—because she couldn't seem to stop being intrigued by him, and she wanted to feel what it would be like to be the object of his scrutiny.

To have him hold her the way he'd held one of those items, to look at her with that intense interest.

"Lady Sophronia, are you interested?"

Sophronia gulped at all the ideas that put into her head, but didn't think Mrs. Green meant to ask any of what Sophronia was mentally answering.

Although the answer to all the questions was "Yes."

"Yes, Mrs. Green, I am."

Mrs. Green smiled thinly, as though wishing Sophronia had said she was too old and tired and determined to remain a spinster for the rest of her life to play any holiday games.

Or it could be that Sophronia was imagining all that.

"I am delighted you feel you can participate in these humorous games, my lady. I would not have thought someone with your interests would want to do something so frivolous."

Or she wasn't imagining it at all.

"My Sophy is quite playful, actually," James said. "She has too intricate a personality to be understood at first or even second meeting. It took me many weeks before I was able to peel back the layers and expose the woman underneath."

Sophronia felt her cheeks—and lots of other parts of her—start to heat at his words. *Peel back the layers and expose her.*

Well, so much for not thinking about all of that. About all of him.

The worst part was she wanted him to peel back her layers and expose her, even though it would only be for a short time, and they both understood that.

Did that make it possible? That it was by necessity short-lived? And how did one broach such a topic? *Excuse me, my pretend betrothed, but do you think we could pretend we were actually betrothed, so we could engage in things that actual betrothed couples do?*

It would take someone far better with words to formulate that thought without seeming like an idiot.

Even her father wouldn't have been able to do it, not that she would have asked for his help with *that.* He was a tolerant parent, but she had to guess he would draw the line at finding the right language so that she could embark on a meaningless but also meaningful limited-time relationship.

Now her head hurt with it all. She hoped they weren't playing Dictionary tonight; she'd probably end up with definitions like "Thingy that does things" or "The opposite of dumb."

Or "Inappropriately obsessed with a tall charming man."

Jamie had to restrain himself, not for the first time, from just taking his fake betrothed and his mother and leaving. But his mother would be disappointed, and what was more, these were the people with whom she socialized—he'd be long gone, but she'd be here to deal with the aftermath of his behavior.

So he did what he could, but felt the prickles of disdain Mrs. Green shot toward Sophronia. All the young ladies, including Miss Green, seemed to understand that he was no longer available, but it appeared that Mrs. Green took it as a personal affront—and perhaps a challenge—that he had arrived encumbered with a wife-to-be.

Although that just gave him more of an excuse to be alone with her, so perhaps he should thank Mrs. Green and her unpleasant behavior.

Meanwhile, he'd be damned if he or Sophronia would be forced into an uncomfortable situation.

"Mrs. Green, if I may, I have a suggestion for a game we could play." He donned his most charming smile, as though he didn't wish her to hell.

"Yes, Mr. Archer?"

"It has been a few years since my mother and I celebrated the holidays together, and one game we used to play is You're Never Dressed Without a Smile. I thought that would be fun."

"Oh, excellent suggestion, Mr. Archer," Miss Green's daughter said, making him less annoyed she'd interrupted the potential kiss he had yet to get. "Mother, I do love that one."

"You'll have to tell us how to play," the vicar whatever-his-name said. "I am not familiar with it."

"Mr. Archer?" Mrs. Green's tone, as usual, made it clear what she wanted to happen. In this case, for him to explain the directions.

"Yes, well, one person is It, and tries to make everyone else in the room smile. The first person to smile then becomes It. At the end, the last remaining person who hasn't smiled wins the game. Simple, really."

He allowed himself to glance over at Sophronia, intrigued to see her cheeks flushed pink and a bright light in her eyes. Ah, so it seemed his Sophy liked to play games, as well.

That added yet another layer to his depth of knowledge about her. Layers, like the ones he'd said he'd peeled away from her, just a few moments ago.

And he would like to do that. Very much.

It wasn't just the missed kiss opportunity that was piquing his interest; it was how she asked him what he felt about the objects in the abbey, and how she paid attention to him as he spoke about what he saw. As though she were truly engaged and interested, not merely being polite.

Even though she was, absolutely, and perfectly, polite.

Perhaps he should have suggested Hide and Go Seek, and then he could have found out for himself just how impolite she was willing to be.

Or no; perhaps later on in the visit, when they had gotten to know one another better. That would be something to look forward to, a prickle of anticipation to help steady his course.

"That sounds delightful," Mrs. Green replied in a voice that indicated it was anything but. Perhaps she just always spoke that way? That would make him very sorry for Mr. Green, although that gentleman didn't seem to mind things one way or the other.

It was after dinner, and the party had all moved into the drawing room, which was arranged for general entertainment—a piano in one corner, several couches scattered about, and a few shelves of books. They hadn't yet started playing the games since there was tea to be had first.

"My Jamie is so clever, don't you think?" Mrs. Archer leaned over to speak in Sophronia's ear, as though sharing a secret, and not something that everyone in the room knew Mrs. Archer thought.

She really was a sweet woman. "He is."

"I am so pleased you'll be joining our family. It's just been me and Jamie for years now, and he deserves some happiness."

And now she felt like the worst kind of lowly worm, fooling this lovely, gentle woman.

"James isn't in town that often, is he?"

Mrs. Archer shook her head regretfully. "No, he is always going off to one place or another. It's been the same ever since he was small. I'd send him out to play, and then he'd end up in the village, or down at the lake, or in the fields. We lived in the country until Jamie was about twelve years old. Then his father—Mr. Archer, that is—found he was required to be at his place of business every day, and so he moved us into London." She sighed. "Jamie takes after his father. My late husband was always off doing things until we got married."

It was on the tip of Sophronia's tongue to ask if James had

any brothers and sisters, but she had to think that a normal
about-to-be-married couple would have discovered that kind
of information about one another already, and while Mrs.
Archer did not appear to be a suspicious type of person, her
suspicions would certainly be aroused if the topic of family
hadn't come up already.

She could, however, safely ask Mrs. Archer questions
about herself. "Do you like living in London?"

Mrs. Archer glanced around as though to ensure nobody
was listening in. They weren't; prior to the start of the games,
Mrs. Green had insisted that James examine yet another arti-
fact—or "arty fact"—and Miss Green had dutifully brought
it out from one room or another for him to see, as well as for
the guests, presumably, to admire, as well.

To Sophronia's eyes, it appeared to be a misshapen drab
piece of pottery. She would not be sharing her opinion with
Mrs. Green.

"I don't really enjoy London," Mrs. Archer said. "That is, I
do like the conveniences, and when Jamie returns to England
he invariably has business in London, so there is a greater
chance I will be able to see him. I do miss him." She sighed
and looked over to where her son was staring intently at the
misshapen drab. "I did always hope—well, it's foolish."

"What did you hope for?" Sophronia asked, wanting to
know even as she was dreading the answer—it would likely be
something involving her son staying nearby with his wife and
their brood of not-yet-existing children.

"I always hoped that when Jamie settled down he would
truly settle down. Like his father did with me. Perhaps in
the country, a town like this one, or like the one where we

lived before. A place where I could see him, and his wife," she added, with a warm smile toward Sophronia, "and where it was less of a commotion."

She was right to have dreaded the answer. It was precisely what she would have imagined the woman wanted, and precisely opposite what her son was determined to do.

She did feel terrible for the deception, but on the other hand, she could feel just how bound up and stifled it made him feel to be in one place for too long.

"I understand that," she replied. "I've always lived in London, and so I am accustomed to it, but I am finding it quite pleasurable to be here in a much quieter place for a while. Even though of course there are plenty of things to do, and plenty of entertainment. But it feels more peaceful, despite the party."

Mrs. Archer beamed at her, as though she had said something entirely clever. When Sophronia had just spoken what was in her heart—she did like it out here, she liked the quiet, and the soft stillness that settled over the place in the evening.

"It is time for the game," James said, addressing them. The misshapen drab seemed to have been put away. He stood in front of them, his expression soft and warm as he looked at his mother. Sophronia felt her heart ache, just a little. She couldn't look at her father any more, even though for some months after he'd died, and she'd discovered how he'd left things, she'd wished he were there so she could rail at him.

But as time had gone on, she'd realized she would be fine, no matter that he hadn't quite taken care of her that way. He had taken care of her by letting her know she was loved, and cared for (at the time), and he respected her opinions and feelings.

She missed him. And she felt regretful that Mrs. Archer would not be her mother-in-law in truth, since she wished she could have that again.

"I will just watch, you know I laugh immediately anyway," Mrs. Archer said, waving her hand at her son. "You are so clever, I was just saying that to your beloved Sophronia here."

His gaze traveled to her, a knowing smile quirking his lips. "My beloved Sophronia has yet to discover just how clever I can be," he said, and it sounded as though he were talking about far more than just a game. Sophronia's breath caught, and she felt her cheeks flush—again—and her heart flutter just a bit in her chest.

He held his hand out as he spoke, and she took it, nearly gasping as she felt the strength of his grip and the heat of his fingers through his gloves. She stood on shaky legs, and smoothed her gown, his keeping hold of her hand all the while.

"Let us play," he said, that grin deepening.

Tuant:

1. Cutting, biting, keen, trenchant.
2. A meringue flavored with almond.
3. Careful, precise.

CHAPTER TEN

Jamie won, of course, as she could have predicted. He'd been so infectiously charming everyone had to laugh, even Mrs. Green, eventually.

And no one had been able to get him to even crack a smile. Sophronia was surprised to find how competitive she'd been at the game, trying her best to make him at least smile.

But no. He remained implacable, a startling change from the charming man she'd come to expect.

She would have to challenge him to a private game of it sometime, perhaps, to see if she could break his composure.

And wasn't that a thought she should absolutely not be having.

"What are you thinking about, my lady?" Maria asked her, pausing midstroke as she was brushing her hair.

Sophronia felt her cheeks immediately begin to burn, and she swallowed. "Nothing. Not a thing." *No need to say it again, Sophronia*, she heard her father's voice say. "Why do you ask?"

Maria shrugged, beginning to brush her hair again. "Because you made this funny noise, and then you looked all different for a second."

Wonderful. So when she thought about things like that, she made funny noises and faces. Maybe that would be the thing to make him laugh.

"What are you doing tomorrow?"

Whatever Mrs. Green wants, Sophronia thought. "I believe we are spending the day at the house, making plans for Christmas. The Greens host a party for the villagers, and so everyone comes and has wine, and food, and there is singing and some dancing."

It sounded delightful, especially since Sophronia had attended very few parties in her life. But also sad, since it meant the visit and the charade would be almost over, and she would be heading to her cottage with Maria, taken care of, but not cared for.

"That sounds a treat," Maria said, her tone showing only delight at the prospect. "And there is that one gown that is perfect for the party—it is cream-colored, with dark green ribbons, and you will look perfect for the season."

"Thank you, Maria, I have no doubt you will make me look lovely." She had to admit to enjoying the look in her pretend betrothed's eye when she appeared dressed in one of her new gowns. She'd never realized before just how much some fabric, buttons, and stitching could alter a person's appearance. Yet another benefit to this whole lying-to-a-perfectly-nice-woman-because-her-son-couldn't-tell-her-the-truth thing.

And with that depressing thought, Sophronia dismissed

Maria and took herself off to bed, trying not to count the remaining days.

"Do you ever lose?" Sophronia—his Sophy—sounded entirely disgruntled. They had been at the Greens for close to a week, with only a week and a few days left to go in the visit.

Jamie didn't think he'd ever spent so much time just socializing. And since it was with all the same people, he'd run out of things to say by about the third day, which meant he was reduced to playing games so he wouldn't die of boredom.

Plus he was, as his pretend betrothed had soon discovered, very good at games.

They had escaped the drawing room after dinner, when Mrs. Green had decided anyone with musical talent had to perform. Jamie had none, and was delighted to discover that neither did Sophy. Another thing they had in common.

They'd told their dismissive hostess that they would prefer to read, so here they were in the library.

Not reading.

Instead, they sat at either end of one of the sofas in the room, him with his legs crossed and leaning back against the sofa, while she sat perfectly straight, her hands placed just so in her lap.

He'd thought he might have tired of looking at her—he tended to tire of things far more quickly than other people did. But he hadn't. If anything, he wanted to look at her more, to see the range of emotions that flittered across her face in the course of minutes.

"I've lost," he said, knowing his saying it so self-righteously would irk her.

She rolled her eyes. "You might have lost, once, but it wasn't to me." She lifted her head in that goddess pose he was coming to adore. "I am not accustomed to losing." Then she shrugged. "Although to be fair, these are not the games I've played in the past. Still," she said, and he wanted to laugh at her aggrieved expression, "it does not seem fair that I have lost each and every game we have played."

"You were so close when we were playing Similes." He shook his head mockingly. "But then you had to say it was strong as a mule, when it's an ox. Mules are the stubborn ones."

She frowned, twisting her mouth up in an expression of disgruntlement. "I could have sworn it was a mule, not an ox."

"What games are you accustomed to playing?" he asked, tilting his head to look at her.

He could hear the strains of music coming from the drawing room, and knew they had some time before anyone would notice they hadn't returned with their books. He was finding that was a good thing—perhaps the only good thing—about a house party, is that the rules were just slightly more relaxed out here, so chaperones weren't always required, and besides, he was engaged to be married.

That is, he was purportedly engaged to be married.

Her expression got dreamy, as though she were recalling a memory. "My father and I played Similes, but we usually made ourselves extend beyond England. In fact, it was a rule that we couldn't use any similes that were in the common vernacular."

"Sounds . . . edifying." He couldn't keep himself from sounding skeptical.

She rolled her eyes again. "Of course it wasn't that, it wasn't as though we deliberately sat around and made ourselves seem important because of our obscure knowledge."

"Good to know," he replied, sounding dubious.

She was about to roll her eyes again, he could tell, but then she paused, and instead, she got a wicked smile on her face.

That smile promised many things, and he hoped he would be the recipient of at least a few of them.

Actually, of all of them.

"I have thought of a game we could play where I will win." She sounded so certain he couldn't help but be intrigued. As though he weren't entirely intrigued already.

"What game?"

"You're Never Dressed Without a Smile." She accompanied her words with, of course, a smile. That same wicked one that promised all sorts of things, probably three-quarters of which she wouldn't know herself.

He would like the chance to teach her, however.

"We played that, and I won. We played a few times, didn't we?" He tapped his mouth with his index finger. "And I believe I won every time." He lowered his hand and looked at her, lifting one eyebrow as he spoke. "Why would tonight's game be any different?"

Why would tonight's game be any different? She hoped he wouldn't regret asking that, since the game she intended to play—that she intended to play with him—would be very different indeed.

She swallowed, feeling her eyes flutter closed for a moment as she braced herself. Not that what was about to occur was unpleasant—it would hopefully be the opposite of that—but that she had never been so forward before. And she was planning on it this evening.

"Because the game will be played with just us," she replied. She scooted closer to him on the sofa, keeping her eyes on his face. His handsome, commanding, far-too-gorgeous-for-her face, only it was also his clearly-interested-she-wasn't-stupid face.

She just hoped the interested section of him trumped the out-of-her-league section.

Now she definitely had his interest. She felt herself exhale, just a bit, out of relief. His expression had tightened, sharpened somehow, and she was keenly, even more so, aware that they were in the library alone, that Mrs. Green and her group of Somewhat Talented Musicians were still playing away in the other room, and this—whatever this was—was going to happen.

One way or the other.

"And how do you think to make me smile, much less laugh?" he asked in a serious tone. She could tell he was schooling himself not to smile, but the glint in his blue eyes belied his sober mien.

"I will just have to say a few words," she said in a low voice.

"And if I don't smile? What then?"

She shrugged, a far more casual gesture than her internal

emotions warranted. "Then you may claim a forfeit. Whatever you want, I will do. If you win, that is."

"Oh, that sounds promising." The combination of his low, sensual tone and the serious expression on his face made something inside of her warm, as though he were touching her all over, a caress that was heating her up from the inside.

But perhaps he didn't mean the way he sounded—she couldn't assume, it wasn't as though she had ever been in this dangerous flirting situation before. For all she knew, he was like this with every lady, regardless of how he thought of her.

Actually, he was like this with every lady. She'd seen it for herself, only there was something slightly different, more intense, about him now. She continued. "For example, I could ensure Miss Green was occupied for a few hours so her mother wouldn't require you to escort her to view more arty facts." She pronounced it as his mother would, and he nearly broke then, as well. "Or if you wanted me to gaze at you in rapt adoration as you expounded on the history of one of those odd jugs you seem to find entrancing. I could do that."

His lips twitched, but he didn't break. "Or I could ask for something else entirely." She shivered at the low promise in his tone.

"What would you want?"

He paused, his expression still serious, but the light in his eyes was fierce and wild. Thrilling her, even though she had no idea what it meant.

"I want a kiss."

She nearly laughed aloud at the irony of it, but merely nodded and thrust her hand out. "We have a deal."

He took her hand, sliding his fingers over her palm, making her heart race with just the merest touch.

Imagine what would happen to her when they did kiss. Because they would be kissing, of that she was now certain.

"You mentioned you could beat me with just a few words." He still held her hand, his tone teasing, his expression entirely somber. "What words would those be?"

She paused and licked her lips, which had suddenly gone dry. His gaze fastened on her mouth and she felt it as though it was an almost palpable touch.

"I want a kiss."

Smicker:

1. The collar of an apron.
2. To look amorously.
3. The spines of a fish.

CHAPTER ELEVEN

Of course he had to smile at that, but it didn't matter, since—since now it was a moot point. "Well, then who is the winner here?" he asked, moving forward to put his hand on her waist.

Drawing her to him, as he'd wanted to do from the first time—well, no, the first time he saw her she'd been sitting down in a pub drinking ale, he hadn't been thinking about what he wanted to do to her, or with her, until a few hours later.

Still, it was fairly close to the first time they'd met.

She leaned back and gazed up at him, and once again, he had cause to be grateful she was such a tall woman. He would only have to lower his mouth to hers a few inches, especially if she rose up on her toes. Kissing could be damned hard on the spine, he'd found, if the two participants were upright.

"Why, I have won, of course. You smiled." And then she did the same, her lips curling up into the most provocative, compelling smile he'd ever seen.

Or that could be just her.

"So will you claim your reward, my lady?" Jamie said, sliding his palm to the small of her back and pulling her closer.

She raised her hands and put them at his shoulders, pushing him back. The immediate words of apology began to come from his mouth, but she shook her head, keeping her gaze locked on his face. "*I* wish to claim my reward, sir," she replied, stressing the first word. "*You* will just have to give it."

Oh, well then. He wanted her to take it more than he'd wanted anything in his entire life. He'd never been with a woman like her before, one who knew what she wanted, even though he was fairly certain she wasn't entirely aware of what she wanted, being an unmarried woman and all. And since he had been with experienced unmarried women before, he knew she wasn't experienced, not at all.

"Will this be your first kiss?" The words popped out of his mouth before he could even think about them.

Her cheeks pinked, and he knew the answer before she spoke. "Yes," she said in a soft voice, her fingers beginning to caress his shoulders.

"Good." He couldn't help the note of masculine pride in his voice. "I will just allow you to take it." He stilled himself, letting his hands go down by his side, watching her as she prepared herself.

God, her face was so expressive. He could watch it for hours, and still find new emotions revealed there. Her eyes swept down his body, almost as though she were touching him everywhere she looked. She allowed her hands to slide down his arms, to his waist. When they came to rest there, she bit her lip, and he had to restrain himself from bending down to bite it, as well.

And then she looked up at him, the frank desire in her eyes making him feel as though he were lit from inside. An odd way to put it, to be sure, but it felt as though only she could make him warm. Could soothe him with her kiss.

Even though he doubted very much that kissing her would be a soothing activity. Exciting, sensual, and an entirely new experience, yes, but not soothing.

"Well?" he said at last. It was speak or claim her mouth, and he knew she didn't want that.

"Don't rush me," she said in nearly a growl. That made him laugh, too—that his polite goddess could be so transformed by the prospect of a mere kiss.

But it wouldn't be just mere, would it. This would be an epic kiss, if he knew his goddess.

He saw her throat work, and she lifted her face to his, raising herself up with the hands at his waist. That necessitated her to move in closer, and he felt the points of contact between them—her hands, his waist, her breasts, his chest.

Their feet.

But he stopped thinking about any of that when she placed her mouth on his. Her kiss was soft and warm, just a simple pressing of their mouths together.

And then she opened her mouth, just a bit, and he did as well, hoping that while she didn't have direct experience with the act that she would have investigated what could happen when one person kissed another.

And, thankfully, it seemed she was a studious person.

Her tongue touched his mouth hesitantly, just the slightest touch, but it was enough to make him groan. Which seemed to encourage her, since she slid her tongue inside his mouth, widening her lips.

The sensation of getting lost in her kiss grew, and it felt as though that was all he could think about, her there, and him here, and them kissing. At that moment, he couldn't say he wanted anything more.

Well, he did—he was a man, after all—and if this was all it ever was, it would be enough.

But he did want more, he had to admit.

Which was why he was the one to eventually draw back, knowing if he didn't that he would reach the point of no return, and he didn't want her first kiss to be also her first other things.

Well, he did, he was a man, after all, but it wouldn't be right.

All of which meant that he was entirely and thoroughly befuddled.

"How was it?" He had to ask; he was a—well, damn it, he knew what he was.

Her eyes were soft and dreamy, but held a sensual glint that made his breath catch. "It was excellent." Her mouth—that mouth he'd just been kissing—twisted into a smirk, as though she were sharing a private joke. With herself. "Delightful. Incredible. *Sensational*, even. An excellent gift," she added in a lower voice.

"All those things, all together?" Jamie leaned in close to whisper in her ear. "Imagine just how stupendous it will be when we do it again."

When we do it again. Goodness, she wanted to do it again, and she wished she could do it again right now, only that would lead, she well knew, to all sorts of improprieties, improper even if they were actually betrothed and not fakely betrothed.

Fakely is not a word, Sophronia, her father muttered somewhere inside her head.

Now is not the time to be offering word critique, Father, she replied.

"Shall we return to the party?" James glanced over her shoulder. "We've been away long enough to miss the music, I believe. Let's just hope they don't ask us what books we've been reading."

She grinned, and turned her head to look at the books on the shelves. "I'll tell them I read a few husbandry guides, paying particular attention to the Husband Husbandry Guide."

He spun and looked at the shelves, his mouth dropping open. "There is no such thing—is there?"

She burst out laughing at his expression, which was equal parts nonplussed and bemused. She shook her head and patted him on the arm. "No, there is no such thing. Although I imagine if there were such a guide, Mrs. Green would have a say in writing it."

"The woman does like to offer pronouncements, doesn't she?" he replied in a rueful tone.

"And potential brides. Thank goodness you had the forethought to provide yourself with a betrothed, or else you would be addressing Mrs. Green as Mother."

She laughed even more when she saw him shudder.

"For that, I should buy you two cottages."

He took her arm and led her out of the library, the glow of the kiss fading as she thought about what he'd said. Of course. There was only this, this brief period of time. An interlude during the holidays. It wasn't as though this was anything more than what it was—two people entering into a bargain to save their respective futures. Their separate respective futures.

At least she now knew he was justified in going to such lengths to prevent an accidental betrothal—she had no doubt but that Mrs. Green, or one of the other ladies, would have him plighting his troth by the time Christmas came around.

And after the holiday, long after the Yule log was burnt down, and the kissing bough had given up all its berries, when the mistletoe had shriveled, and the snow was just a distant memory, she would be snug in her cottage with Maria, with memories of this night, and that kiss, to warm her through the ensuing years.

That should be enough. It would be enough. And perhaps, if she was patient, and open, she would find someone who would truly wish to be betrothed to her. To marry her, and stay in one place, and always be reliable, and have enough money to keep her in books and ale. That was all she wanted. Just someone to belong to in a place she felt she belonged.

If she were to receive that Christmas gift one year—not this year, of course, but someday—she would rejoice and try to forget about the tall, restless man who offered her a chance at escape. As well as her first kiss.

"You're not regretting this, are you?" he asked in a low voice as they walked down the hall to the drawing room.

"No, of course not, why?" She glanced up at him, noting the concern in his eyes. "Are you?" *Dear God, please don't let him regret this.* That would be the worst Christmas gift, the anti-Christmas gift, and she herself would regret not making her way to her cousin and his children and the all the chicken iterations, and if she—

"That kiss was the best thing to occur since my mother informed me we'd be attending a house party." She couldn't doubt the sincerity in his tone. "It is just—you sighed, just then, as though something were weighing on you." Right. She had forgotten how observant he was.

I was just thinking about how this would all come to an end, and Cinderella would get a cottage, not a prince, at the end of the story.

"I think I was just dreading more of Mrs. Green's orders. Imagine what else she might want us to do while we're here."

He grinned, with such a devilish look in her eye she nearly swooned. "We'll have to excuse ourselves to go play some of our own games."

Forget thinking beyond now, when she'd be off with Maria in a simple cottage paid for with his money. For once, she was going to live in the moment. She would enjoy what this time now would bring, and figure out the rest later.

She could return to being a responsible woman who looked to the future in a week or so; for now, she was as careless and headstrong and impulsive as the next person.

Who happened to be him.

Matutinal:

1. Of, relating to, or occurring in the morning.
2. Feeling nauseated.
3. An acrimonious parting.

Chapter Twelve

He didn't know what he had done, just that he had done something. Besides being kissed by her, that is.

He wanted to inquire more, but they had only a few moments between the library and the drawing room, and he didn't want to get into a discussion where anybody could see them.

It worried him; he couldn't tell what she was thinking now. Her face looked as though someone had drawn a curtain down, her usual lively expression dimmed.

They stepped back into the drawing room, her slightly ahead of him, his hand at the small of her back, just grazing the fabric of her gown with his knuckles. He wished they hadn't ever left the library, that they were still there, kissing, or her teasing him about books and their laughing together.

"Jamie, you have been an age! What could you and Sophronia have gotten up to for so long?"

His mother didn't mean to be shocking, of course; she never did. But all the same, most of the rest of the party smothered chuckles, except for Mrs. Green, who glowered.

She might be the most unpleasant woman he had ever met, but at least she was consistently unpleasant.

"As you are well aware, Mother, I am fascinating when I want to be." He assisted Sophronia into a chair beside his mother. "And my betrothed finds me infinitely fascinating. Don't you, Sophy?"

He grinned at her, hoping she would burst out laughing or say something cutting in response. But she merely lifted a brow and nodded, biting her lip. To stifle a laugh, or a rebuttal? And why was he feeling so torn up about what her reaction might possibly be?

"We were just discussing the plans for tomorrow," the viscountess said. "Mrs. Green has suggested we make a game of finding a suitable tree for decorating. The team who finds the best tree has the honor of—well, what does the team have the honor of doing, Mrs. Green?"

The lady surveyed the house party with a considering air. "The winning team members will be allowed to stand under the mistletoe with the person of their choosing."

Not bad, Mrs. Green, not bad at all. He would have to make sure he or Sophy won, just so he would have the privilege of kissing her in front of all these people.

Of staking his claim to her, even though they both knew— and only they knew—that the claim was a temporary one.

But meanwhile, he didn't know if he could wait until tomorrow to kiss her again, now that he'd tasted the sweetness of her lips, and felt how she responded to him.

Actually, he did know if he could wait. And the answer was no, he couldn't.

The knock came just after Maria had gone, leaving Sophronia in blissful anticipation of a comfortable book, a warm fire, and an hour before she thought she should try to be in bed.

Thankfully, Mrs. Green's dictatorial ways extended to telling her guests when they should be tucked up in their rooms, and the lady insisted everyone get a good night's sleep since the holiday tree-hunting expedition was likely to be strenuous.

Sophronia didn't argue since it meant more time away from the lies they were telling, and Mrs. Archer, whom Sophronia found she liked more each time they were together.

Yes, the woman was talkative, and somewhat silly, but she had such a good heart, and she loved her son so much, even if she didn't entirely understand him.

It made Sophronia feel even more terrible that she and Mrs. Archer's son were lying to her face, and she knew that Mrs. Archer would be devastated when she learned that Sophronia had died. Even though it hopefully wouldn't be true.

But that wasn't answering the door, was it?

Of course she knew who it was on the other side; it wasn't as though there was anyone else at the house who would be knocking at eleven o'clock at night. She walked to the door, tightening her wrapper but still feeling dangerously underdressed.

Not because he would necessarily get carried away, but because she would. She definitely had not expected that kiss to be so . . . meaningful. Important. Wonderful.

Yes, many words for describing one thing. As seemed to be the case when she thought about him, or that, or how this holiday was both the most wonderful and the most painful one she'd ever had.

She pulled the lock and opened the door, stepping aside to let him in. He wasn't dressed for sleeping, as she was, but he was more casually clothed than before—he had removed his cravat and coat, and wore only his shirt and trousers. He had his hands full with something, but she didn't notice that, because she was too distracted—now that his cravat was off, she could see his strong neck and a few tufts of hair peeking over the collar of his shirt.

Those hairs made her feel all sorts of new and strange feelings.

"What are you doing here?" Because she was fairly certain he wasn't here so she could admire the hair on his chest.

He grinned and held up what was in his hands—two glasses and a bottle of wine. "I'm here to strategize how we're going to win the tree-finding contest tomorrow."

She gave him a skeptical look. "And for that we need wine?"

He shook his head and strode past her to place the wine and glasses on her bedside table, then sat down on the bed. Her bed. "The wine isn't for strategizing, Sophycakes, it's for fun." He paused, then a sly grin twisted his lips. "We do know how to have fun together, don't we?"

Sophronia immediately felt her face turn not pink, but thoroughly and absolutely red. She doubted a sunset at the end of a summer day was more red than she was at this moment.

He was watching her, and his grin turned into full-out laughter, but not as though he was enjoying her discomfiture, but as though he was gleeful about it all. About his being here, and them together, and their kiss from earlier before.

She could do this, hadn't she vowed to give herself permission to have fun? She went and plopped next to him on the bed, the motion pushing them together. "Well, open that bottle, then, and let's strategize."

H̲e didn't think he had ever laughed so much in his entire life. His Sophronia—not Sophycakes, she'd informed him in a mockingly supercilious tone—turned out to be even more fun when he was alone with her.

That is, even more fun when he was alone with her and not kissing her. He still thought kissing her was just slightly more fun than making elaborate plans to lure their competitors to a sparse bit of forest. Not that they knew where said sparse bit of forest was, nor how they would succeed in luring the others there, but they had a stupidly fun time talking about it.

"And then, when you've done your job and brought them to where they're all somewhere else, I'll fell the best tree and drag it back to the house."

She looked at him askance. "All by yourself?"

Jamie felt the sting of masculine pride. "You don't believe I can handle a tree on my own?"

She took the last swallow of her wine, and he poured her another glass. "No, I don't."

He reached for her glass and set it on the table, then took her hand and put it on his bicep. And flexed.

At which point, her eyes widened, and his masculine pride was assuaged. But now other parts of him wished to be assuaged—namely, to have her run her hands all over him, not just on his arm.

"Uh," she said, not letting go. If anything, squeezing harder.

It was difficult to keep his muscle flexed for so long, but if it kept that wondrous look on her face, he'd do it.

"Have I rendered you speechless?" he asked, feeling rather at a loss for words himself. Mostly because his mouth would prefer to be doing something else.

She scowled and dropped her hand from his arm, but then launched herself at him, knocking them both over onto the bed. She lowered her mouth to his and kissed him, this time with much more finesse than the first time.

His Sophycakes was a fast learner, it seemed.

He allowed her to take what she so obviously wanted, opening his mouth to let her tongue in, reaching his arm across her body and letting his hand rest just below her breast on her rib cage. Although that was not, technically, what she wanted, but he figured that if he wanted it, it was a likely thing she did, as well.

And oh, how he wanted it.

Clothed in her sleepwear, she was less unapproachable goddess and more . . . approachable. Although that was an inane thought, given that they were each doing plenty of approaching at this very moment.

She twisted so she was nearly underneath him, her hand

caressing his back, her other hand in his hair. He felt her softness everywhere, and it was more amazing than he would have imagined.

So amazing, in fact, that he had to stop before it was too late, and they were betrothed in truth.

He reluctantly broke the kiss, hearing their gasping breaths in the otherwise silent room.

"What is it?" she said, a dazed look in her eye.

He knew how she felt.

"If we don't stop, we might never stop, and then—" He paused, not quite sure how to phrase it.

"You'll feel worse about killing me off?" she said in a dry voice.

He laughed, albeit somewhat uncomfortably. Being with her had ameliorated his restless spirit, for certain, but he still felt the pull of the unknown, of continually moving so he didn't have to settle down. Or be anything more than he was.

Was that enough? Would it always be enough?

Or was there something more? Something . . . different that was possible?

Images of his father, how he'd just sat on the sofa and drank wine—rather as Jamie was doing tonight, although on a bed, not a sofa—crowded his brain, making him acutely aware that this might lead him to that very same dissatisfied spot.

He rolled over onto his back, his body immediately regretting the loss of her. Well, his brain did as well, but his brain also shied away from that fact.

"It's just I don't wish to—" he began, only to have her cut him off.

"I know. I wouldn't think you meant anything by it." She gave a half laugh. "Besides which, it was me who made the first charge. None of this," she said, and waved her hands in the air, "means anything. I know that. It's just"—and he heard how her breath caught, and his throat thickened—"it's just that it feels so wonderful." She laughed softly. "And wondrous, and amazing, and all sorts of other words I've likely never heard of."

He rolled onto his side, propping his head in his hand. She turned her head to look at him, and they were so close, he could see her brown eyes had flecks of green and gold within, and there was a very faint mole on her eyelid.

He wanted to kiss that mole. And everywhere else on her face.

"I feel the same way," he said softly, surprised to find it was true. He'd never been with a woman who intrigued him as much when he was not doing inappropriate things with her as when he was.

"But I know I can't have you forever," she said. "Nor would I want to," she added quickly, once again stirring up Jamie's masculine pride. "I know you are restless, and I—I just want a place to belong."

He wished he could give that to her. But he knew himself, and what's more, he knew what she wanted—a cottage somewhere, a cottage he'd promised he'd give her when they'd entered into their bargain.

That sounded like slow death to him—staying in the same place, knowing the same people, seeing the same things.

It was better this way. It *was*.

He looked at her for a moment longer, then got off the bed

and stood, gazing down at her. Her face was still flushed, her lips red and swollen, and he wished he were enough of a cad to take what she would likely give him, if he coaxed her.

But he wasn't, and so she wouldn't, and therefore he should go before the temptation of her outweighed the honor of him.

"Good night, Sophronia," he said, then turned on his heel and walked quickly out the door, before he had the chance to change his mind.

Uhtceare:

1. The next-to-last toe.
2. The combination of juniper and mint, used as a remedy for toothache.
3. Anxiety experienced just before dawn.

Chapter Thirteen

Sophronia flopped back on the bed, feeling all sorts of new, interesting, and very difficult emotions. At the same time.

Why did he have to be so honorable? Why couldn't he just make the decision for her, push her to where she secretly wished to be?

The one man with whom she wanted to be inappropriate, and he turned out to be an honorable, considerate man. Of all the stupid luck.

She had to laugh at herself, of course, because if she didn't—well, if she didn't, she'd cry. And she did not want to cry. Not only because crying felt so maudlin, but also because it would make her eyes puffy, and her nose red, and Mrs. Green would likely notice and comment and send her daughter scurrying after Jamie to try and comfort the poor dear.

And then he'd end up compromising Miss Green, and have to really marry her, not just be pretend betrothed to her.

So crying was not on the agenda.

It had felt so wonderful, being kissed by him. She'd liked how he felt, as well, his muscles, his back, his mouth on hers.

And now she was back to wishing he weren't so honorable.

But if he were so honorable he wouldn't have thought of this devious plan in the first place—she wouldn't be here, they wouldn't have met, and she'd be in the country tending children and chickens. So maybe it was her?

No, she knew it wasn't that. He seemed to have a perverse sense of honor, one that made him try to please his mother (in the short term, at least), but wouldn't have to do anything unpleasant for himself. And it was clear he thought being tied down permanently was thoroughly unpleasant.

Whereas she had to admit that if the person tying her down permanently was him, she would find it very pleasant indeed.

And that was what she had decided earlier, wasn't it? Even if it was temporary—and that wasn't an if, it just was a fact— she would very much like to find out what it would all be like. She could be a respectable spinster when she and Maria were at the cottage.

During this most festive season, she wanted to be festive. She knew now she couldn't depend on him to do the wrong thing, so she was going to have to.

She was going to have to seduce him.

Happy Christmas, indeed.

There would be no seduction today, however. For one thing, it was too cold outside to engage in any proper seduction, and secondly, Jamie was too competitive to get sidetracked by anything that might prevent him from winning.

"Over here, Sophy," he called. They had been the first into

the forest, and he'd had the foresight to equip himself with a sturdy saw and some rope so they wouldn't waste time getting help to drag the tree in.

"Sophronia," she muttered, following the sound of his voice. The wardrobe he'd gotten for her didn't include clothing suitable for tramping about in the cold and the snow, so she was already damp and cross.

And since she couldn't achieve her own ends, now that she'd decided on them, she was even more cross. But it wasn't as though she could say, "Excuse me, James, but would you mind taking advantage of me over by this tree here? Yes, it is inappropriate and scandalous and cold, but I've come to realize that this is what I want for Christmas, and you are the only one who can give it to me."

She *wished* she could say that, but she also suspected that the aforementioned cold and snow would reduce the pleasure she found in it, and if she were going to ruin herself, she wanted it to be enjoyable, at least.

"Look, this has to be the best tree out here," he said in an enthusiastic tone of voice as she made her way to him.

It was definitely a tall tree. Perhaps twice his height, and that was saying something. Its branches were thick and full, and it didn't take much imagination to see the tree would be gorgeous decorated with garland, candles, and ribbon.

Or whatever Mrs. Green deemed appropriate to decorate a tree with. Thank goodness she didn't take issue with Prince Albert's importation of the custom, since Sophronia did love the tradition.

She'd have to keep it up next year, when it was just her and Maria.

Although she wouldn't have six feet plus worth of strong male to haul her tree back for her. She'd have to get a gentle shrub or something.

"Are you certain we can bring it back by ourselves? Oughtn't I go get some help?" Sophronia couldn't keep the skepticism from her voice. It was a very tall tree.

"And risk someone else finding something that would suit just as well, and they would win the contest?" He sounded outraged. "No, we can do it, didn't I prove that last night?"

Oh, right. By taking her hand and placing it on his bicep, which was hard and large and made her feel all sorts of prickly things inside.

"You did." No need to express her continued doubt. He would likely just hoist the tree over his shoulder to prove her wrong.

"Bring the saw over, I'll have the tree down in no time."

Sophronia handed him the saw, then watched as he started the process.

A half hour later, he was in only his shirtsleeves, his hair was tangled and damp, and he was still sawing.

She didn't think she'd ever seen such a gloriously visceral sight in her life.

"There," he said at last, just in time for her to jump out of the way. The tree landed with a thump, sending whirls of snow flying up into the air.

"Now all we have to do is get it back to the house."

"Good thing that's all we have to do," Sophronia commented dryly.

But she had to admit she was wrong—gloriously, sweatily, strenuously wrong.

He dragged the tree while she walked alongside, holding his jacket and cravat. She felt awash in his scent, a warm, strong aroma that just seemed essentially him.

He'd rolled his sleeves up, and she couldn't stop darting glances at his forearms—strong, of course, and sprinkled with brown hair.

"Let's sing, shall we?" he said, startling her out of her perusal of said arms.

"What? But don't you need your breath to—?"

He shook his head in mock outrage. "You doubt me, Sophycakes. I can drag a tree and sing at the same time. I am very talented."

She had to laugh at that. "Fine, then. What shall we sing?"

"A holiday carol, of course. Have you no imagination?"

I've got plenty, she wanted to reply. *Enough to think about what it would feel like if you wrapped me in those strong arms of yours and kissed me senseless. And did other things I know about, but am too embarrassed to discuss even in the confines of my own brain.*

"Good King Wenceslas looked out, on the Feast of Stephen," he began to sing, and of course he had a lovely voice, all resonant and rich and thrilling.

She joined him, not nearly as shy about singing out loud because it was with him, and he just made her feel so comfortable, even though he also made her feel all prickly and odd and wanting.

"Yes, your tree is definitely the best, Mr. Archer." For once, Sophronia didn't begrudge the woman's definitive way of speaking. It was a few hours later, and Jamie had unfortunately had a bath and gotten properly dressed again. The rest of the party had returned, each team having retrieved a tree for Mrs. Green's inspection.

None were as large or as robust as theirs. Of course. Because none of the team members was as large or as robust as Jamie himself.

"And you may take anyone you wish under the mistletoe," Mrs. Green continued. Jamie glanced her way, a mischievous look in his eye. "Except for your own team member," she added, and Sophronia wanted to laugh at how startled he looked at that, and he looked at her again, only this time it was in shock and a mild expression of horror.

"Mrs. Archer, do come and stand just here," Sophronia said, taking the older woman by the arm and guiding her under the mistletoe.

Jamie met her gaze and smiled, a thankful, relieved smile that made her feel all warm and useful.

"Oh, but what about the other young ladies?" Mrs. Archer expostulated, even though she went to the correct spot willingly enough.

"None are as deserving of a holiday kiss as you, Mother," Jamie replied smoothly, looking down at her fondly. He leaned down and kissed her on the cheek, then shot one last thankful look at Sophronia.

"And now that is done, we will all go rest for a bit and then meet again at dinner. We will have the tree decorated, and then we can play some more games and sing carols." Mrs. Green looked directly at Sophronia. "We all need to look our best."

Thus commanded, Sophronia returned to her bedroom,

thinking about strong forearms, what she wanted to do, and the best way to go about it.

"Not that gown, Maria. The gold one."

Maria's hand stilled in the wardrobe and she darted a glance back at Sophronia. "Are you certain? That one seems rather grand for a house party."

"It isn't as though I will have occasion to wear it any other time, Maria," Sophronia replied in a dry tone of voice. "After this, the most I'll be dressing up for is maybe a village dance, and then only to keep watch over the young ladies."

Maria shook her head. "You never know, my lady. You could be in our cottage and a handsome stranger would stop by, needing something all of a sudden, and there'd you be, and he'd be struck by you, and then you could wear that gown on your wedding day."

Wearing a gown bought by the man who had engaged her to act as his pretend betrothed to marry a stranger she had yet to meet, and doubted existed, didn't sound like the kind of thing she wanted to be doing. Especially since she'd rather be doing all the marrying in the gold gown with the man who had actually purchased the gown in the first place.

She was a hopeless wreck, she knew that. But at least, at the end of it, she would be on her own, beholden only to herself. Ensuring she and Maria had a reasonable future ahead of them.

Huzzah.

But she also had a seduction to accomplish, hence the gold gown. Huzzah!

It was worth all of Maria's shaking her head and concern that she was overdressed to see the expression on his face when she entered the dining room. He had been speaking with Mr. Green, but turned as the door opened, and his mouth dropped open, as well.

He walked quickly to her, taking her elbow in his hand and guiding her to her seat. "You look lovely, Sophy," he murmured, and she knew it wasn't for show, he really meant it, since he'd said it too quietly for anyone else to hear.

"You do, too," she replied. He did, of course; he was dressed in his evening clothes, and his hair was as smooth and well-brushed as she'd ever seen, so she was better able to see his face. There was something appealing about how dangerously rakish he looked when his hair was unruly, but there was also something appealing about him when he was well-groomed, the clean lines of his face showing the result of a close shave, his features standing out in their stark beauty.

In other words, there was something appealing about him no matter what he did to himself. She should just admit that and stop fussing about it.

Dinner was enjoyable, even though Sophronia spent far too much time darting glances at him rather than what was on her plate, so she didn't notice what she'd actually eaten.

Hopefully this was not the time Mrs. Green decided to poison her.

"We will be decorating the trees after dinner, and then

we will play some games. The townsfolk will come tomorrow afternoon to partake of holiday refreshments and we must present them with the best Christmas trees they have ever seen." Mrs. Green's normally disapproving expression was practically beatific. "As happens every year."

Jamie leaned over to whisper in her ear. They were seated in the large room the trees had all been brought to, theirs occupying the place of honor right in front of the fireplace. "If it happens every year, then how can they be the best they've ever seen?"

Sophronia stifled a giggle. "Perhaps you should be the one to bring up that incongruity to her. I don't think she thinks very well of me, given our circumstances."

"For which I am devoutly grateful," Jamie replied, a sincere look in his eye.

The servants, under Mrs. Green's watchful eye—and commanding voice—dragged in all the decorations deemed essential for the trees: candles, ribbons, apples, colored paper, dolls, sweetmeats, and walnuts. At first it seemed as if there were far too many things to fit on the trees, but since their tree was so enormous, it was just enough.

"Goodness," Sophronia breathed, as she stood back and looked at the sight.

It was impressive. The candles had all been lit, casting a golden glow that seemed as bright as the sun. The trees' branches were bedecked with all the treasure, and Sophronia glanced around at the other guests, all of whom were wearing the same enchanted expression.

It was lovely. She couldn't, she wouldn't, think that in half an hour or so the candles would be snuffed. For right now, this was enough. Enough that she was here, drinking in the sight, feeling the charm and the warmth of the season.

Not to mention the charm and the warmth of her fake betrothed, who looked even more gorgeous in the candlelight, the flickering lights making shadows on his face, highlighting the strength of his cheekbones, the dark intensity of his gaze.

Oh, Sophronia, you are in so much trouble. And this will all be a distant memory in a few months, and then next Christmas you'll recall it, hopefully with a warmth and a pang of something to be cherished.

"What games will I be winning at this evening?" Jamie said, viewing the company. Mr. Green was tucked in the corner, drinking a second or third glass of port; the viscountess and her daughter were seated on the sofa, talking about a ball they'd been to where the viscountess's daughter had been, as usual, the prettiest thing there; the vicar had buttonholed Sophronia and was talking animatedly about her father and his own collection of books; and Mrs. Green and her daughter were discussing what to serve to the villagers the next day.

"I like the game Alphabet Minute," Miss Green offered with a hesitant smile. Jamie returned the smile, thinking how difficult it must be to be Mrs. Green's daughter.

"I do, as well," he said. He glanced around the room. "Does everyone who wishes to play know how to play?"

Sophronia shook her head. "I do not, but I don't have to play."

"Don't be silly," he replied. "It's simple. We choose a topic, and then we begin to discuss it, only we have to start each sentence with the next letter in the alphabet. So if we start at the letter G, the next person has to say something beginning with H, and so on."

She still looked puzzled, but shrugged. "I will figure it out, I suppose."

"Yes, you will." His Sophy was clever, she would catch on quickly.

And when had he come to think of her as his Sophy?

"What topic shall we choose?"

Mrs. Green had the answer, of course. "Christmas, naturally. Mr. Archer, you shall begin. The choice of letter is yours."

"Merry Christmas, everyone," he said. He nodded to Miss Green. "The next letter is N."

"No room at the inn is what Mary and Joseph heard on their journey."

"Or was it that there was no *groom* at the inn," Sophy said, shooting him a mischievous glance.

Well-played, he thought, smothering a grin.

"Perhaps we will all get our heart's desire," the viscountess's daughter said with a sly look.

"Queen Victoria might issue a proclamation," the viscountess said.

"Really?"

That was his mother. He was proud she had come up with something so quickly.

"So when you mention the queen, you should also mention her husband."

"That's Prince Albert, is it not?"

"Undoubtedly."

Now it seemed everyone was joining in the game, without regard for whose turn it was. It was actually fun to watch their faces as they thought of a sentence for the letter, and Jamie felt as though he finally understood why a house party of this sort was enjoyable. Not that he wished to do it all the time, but it had its appeal—the camaraderie of good conversation, company, and an overriding belonging to the season that made him feel relaxed, and as though he might not jump out of his skin at any moment.

Or, he thought as he glanced over at her, that was just Sophy's influence.

He had been a gentleman the night before, and while he wasn't precisely regretting that—well, never mind, he was, but he knew it was the right thing to do.

But if she said she wanted to explore further, then who was he to stand in the way of adventure?

He'd just have to let her make the next move in the game.

Cunctation:

1. Procrastination; delay.
2. The inability to pronounce certain consonants.
3. A confused state of mind.

CHAPTER FOURTEEN

What was the protocol for visiting a gentleman by yourself in his bedroom?

Scratch that, there wasn't any such thing. At least not that she knew of; perhaps she should have befriended the viscountess's daughter, it seemed as though she knew far more about such things, the male and female thing, than Sophronia did.

Although nearly anybody would know more than Sophronia, so that didn't signify.

She drew her wrapper around her, tying the knot to close it as she slid her feet into her slippers.

It was nearly one o'clock, and the house had been quiet for over an hour. The games had continued all evening, and they had been fun, she had to admit, but she kept wishing everyone would just get tired so she could get on with what she wanted to do.

With him.

Even thinking about it made her breath catch—and here she was thinking about actually doing it? What if she was unable to breathe entirely? What if she expired in his bedroom from lack of oxygen, and he had to explain to everyone how she came to be there and then she really would be dead, and Mrs. Archer would be sad and Mrs. Green would be delighted and—and—

"Breathe, Sophronia." He'd said that to her when they were just embarking on this masquerade. It was good advice then and it was good advice now.

She stepped into the hallway, thankful that his bedroom was only a few doors down from hers. It was dark, and she didn't want to end up sprawled on the floor because she'd missed her footing.

That would be even awkwarder—for her, at least—than expiring in his bedroom. And yes, she knew that wasn't a word.

She reached his door without either fainting or falling, and counted it as a victory already. And then she raised her hand to knock, but the door whooshed open, and she was pulled inside.

"I was hoping," he began, before lowering his mouth onto hers.

She twined her arms around his neck, remembering to breathe through her nose, wanting to burrow up into his skin and get subsumed in him, his warmth, his scent, his size.

He ran his hands down her back, then right under her buttocks, lifting her off her feet and pressing her to his chest. She gasped, and he chuckled, walking backward before lying down on the bed with her still on his body. As though she weighed nearly nothing.

"I'll smush you," she said, when she was able to lift her mouth.

He smirked at her, his hands still on her arse, his blue eyes alit with what she very much thought was delighted pleasure. "Of course you won't," he said. "Haven't you learned by now that I am much stronger than I look? And if I do say so myself, I already look awfully strong."

His tone was so smug and sure of himself she had no choice but to be amused. And to be certain she wouldn't crush him in her ardor.

"Now what are you doing visiting my bedroom at such a late hour?" He grinned, and she couldn't help but grin back. "Maybe that is the topic for an Alphabet Minute game." He kissed her briefly. "What are you doing here, Miss Sophronia?"

X. The next letter was X, which he knew, the competitive wretch. "Ex-amining the betrothed," she replied.

He shook his head, but didn't challenge her. "You like what you see, then?"

Zed. Whose idea was it to play this game when she could be kissing him? "Zounds, how could I not?" She shifted so she could splay her hand on his chest. His remarkably broad chest.

"A wise choice, my lady," he replied.

"But why are you still talking when you could be kissing me?" There, it was out in the open.

"Consider it done," he replied, pulling her to him so their bodies touched nearly everywhere.

She was here. He'd nearly given up hope that she would come, but here she was. He was relieved he had decided not to chase after her—this would be her choice, not his, just as her wanting a cottage in a small village somewhere was her choice, as well, and it was within his means to give it to her.

But meanwhile, before all that, there was this. The gift of her.

He relished her kiss, plundered her mouth with his tongue as his hands roamed over her curves—she was slender, yes, but she had all the right curves, and those curves fit perfectly in his hands.

She was caressing his chest, running her palm over his nipples, making him want to groan and laugh all at the same time.

And have wonderful sublime sexual relations with her, but that went without saying.

Only he should say something, shouldn't he? It wouldn't be honorable to just assume something because a dressed-for-bed woman had appeared at one's door in the middle of the night?

Damn it. "Are you sure about this?" he said, murmuring into her ear.

She stilled and buried her nose in his neck. *Please say yes, please say yes*, he thought.

And then she licked his skin as her palm continued her travels on his chest, down his side, and at his waist. So close to right there it was maddening and wonderful and excruciating all at the same time.

"Does that answer your question?" she said, accompanying her words with a low laugh.

"Absolutely," he replied, taking her and flipping her onto her back, swallowing her noise of surprise with his mouth.

Part of him—no surprise which part—wanted to just take her, slide his hand up her leg, taking her night rail with it, exposing what he fully anticipated to be long legs.

He'd never been with a woman who was this tall before. In fact, he'd never been with a woman who was this smart, who was this remarkable, who was able to soothe him while at the same time making his heart race and his throat tighten and do other things to other parts of his body.

No surprise which part there, either.

But this wasn't just about him, and it would all be so much sweeter if he took his time.

She was gazing up at him, a warm, sensuous look on her face, less like a goddess now and entirely like a woman. A woman who knew what she wanted, and thankfully, what she seemed to want was him.

"What are you thinking about?" she asked in a husky voice.

Well, he could answer that. "You."

She laughed and swatted his arm. "We have so much in common, I was thinking about you, too. Namely," she continued, arching an eyebrow, "when you were going to get on with it."

That was so entirely unexpected he burst out laughing. He didn't think he'd ever laughed while engaged in all of this sort of activity—a new experience for him, as it would be a new experience for her. Albeit not the same new experience.

"Get on with it?" he repeated. "If you have somewhere to be, please do let me know, and I will hasten the activity." He waggled his eyebrows meaningfully, and she grinned.

"I don't have anywhere to be, but I believe you do," she

said, winking at him. *Winking!* That was even more unexpected than her urging him to just get on with it.

And he didn't know if he should get on with ravishing her, as he dearly wished to do, and it seemed she did, as well, or he wanted to stop and laugh until he cried.

Definitely a new experience.

Sophronia had never felt more daring in her life. Which made sense, since she had never *been* so daring in her life. Not just coming to his room clad in her night rail and wrapper, but encouraging him to—to *do* things she very much wanted him to do to her.

His expression when she urged him to get on with it was delightful—so surprised, and almost affronted that she would dare to issue a command.

"You appear to be this—this regal vision, all elegance and, and regality."

She was touched by his compliment, even though he'd repeated himself.

"But you're not that at all," he continued, leaving Sophronia to wonder just what he was going to say. "You're"—he put his hand on her cheek, his thumb on her mouth, his gaze on her face—"you're clever and impudent and ready for an adventure." He smiled and stroked her mouth. "And I am happy to provide it for you."

And then he kissed her, but he didn't just kiss her, because that would be too weak a word for what he was doing to her. He was imprinting her, claiming her body as his own with every touch. And currently he was touching her waist, his fingers splayed so they were nearly touching her breast, an occurrence she didn't realize had been entirely lacking in her life but now she didn't know how she had lived without it.

Touch me there, she wanted to say, only her mouth was occupied, kissing him back, learning his taste and smell and feel.

She had somehow wrapped her arms around him and was stroking his strong, solid back, pulling him into her, even though he was practically on top of her already.

His—that part was pressed into her, a hard, quite fervent reminder of what was going to happen, or else she would actually expire.

She heard herself moan, low and deep in her throat, her whole body feeling as though it had been zapped with an electric current. Only the electric current was named Jamie, and she hadn't been thoroughly zapped quite yet.

This was the Christmas gift she had really wanted when she thought she wanted a kiss. This—this *ownership*, this entire subsumption into feeling, not thinking at all.

Even though she was thinking. But all she was thinking about was him.

Oh, God, and now his hand was on her breast, his finger rubbing her nipple, causing spirals of a slow, sensuous heat to curl through her body. And his other hand—well, that was drawing her night rail up, his palm on her shin, her knee, her thigh, and then—

She couldn't help but gasp as his fingers reached there, and he broke the kiss, the expression in his eyes both fiercely desiring and concerned. "Are you—is this all right?" he asked, speaking in a ragged voice.

"Mm-hm," she replied, knowing that actual speech might be beyond her. At this moment, at least.

"You're so ready for me," he murmured, his fingers touching her, finding her wet, which would have embarrassed her if she hadn't been so thoroughly determined not to be embarrassed.

Not at this moment, at least; later on, then she could be embarrassed, when she was an old spinster living with her chatty maid in a cottage somewhere. But she would also be able to look back at this whole thing and be delighted that she had been bold enough to say what she wanted, and to get it.

"I am ready." She spoke against his mouth. "So why don't you get on with it?"

He half laughed, half groaned, and she stopped being able to think as he pushed her legs apart and something that was not his hand was at her entrance, and it felt wonderful, if entirely frightening, and made her breathless in all sorts of ways.

Aubade:

1. A jelly made with quince.
2. To lean back.
3. A song or poem greeting the dawn.

CHAPTER FIFTEEN

Had she thought before she might die if he didn't do all this to her?

Now she had to wonder if she would die because he had—of pleasure, of overwhelming emotion, of just feeling glorious and as though the first part of your life was in muted shades of gray, and now the world was colored in the most vivid of hues.

Yes, it hurt at first, and it definitely felt as though it wouldn't entirely fit, but Jamie was patient, even though she could tell it was a strain.

And then, eventually, he thrust home, and she felt him all the way inside, sending echoes of pleasure through her body.

It wasn't just mindless pleasure, either; that is, she felt mindless, but he was mindful, moving carefully and clearly concentrating on how she was feeling, and what felt good.

My goodness, did it feel good.

And it felt as though it were building to something even better.

"That's it, love." He kissed her hard and fierce, and then lowered his head to her neck, his grasp tightening as he continued to thrust, in and out, in a maddeningly wonderful rhythm.

She felt it start to pick her up and sweep her away, knowing it was impossible to stop, not that she would be idiotic enough to stop it at all.

"Ohhh," she said as she felt the escalation making its inexorable way to somewhere, she had no idea.

And then it was as though that same electric current sparked through her, shooting tendrils of pleasure through her entire body, making her boneless and subject to all her feelings and emotions.

She half opened her eyes and saw his smirk of satisfaction, and then he got a look of intense concentration on his face as he increased his rhythm, pushing harder and faster until all she could feel was him, thrusting deep, hearing the sound of their bodies crashing together, his grunts and moans which managed to sound intriguing and not ridiculous.

Until finally, he thrust in and stayed there, his whole body shaking, his hair falling on her face, their bodies touching completely everywhere.

She never wanted to move.

And it seemed, after a few moments, that neither did he.

That would be uncomfortable after an hour or so.

She wriggled a bit under him and he withdrew, rolling onto his side and gasping. "Oh, my lord, Sophycakes." He had his eyes closed, but his face bore a smile.

She had done that to him. Or more accurately, they had done that together and this was the result. "Sophronia," she corrected, hearing the own laughter in her voice.

She wasn't expecting his next words.

"If there is a—a result from this, you will let me know, won't you?" He placed his palm on her stomach, and she gaped at him, not quite sure what he meant, until she did.

Well, that was hardly romantic. Although it was her fault for engaging in it without thinking of the consequences—the result, as he'd put it.

"Yes, of course," she said in a stiff tone of voice.

"Did I upset you?" And now, damn it, he sounded concerned. And she felt like she'd been irresponsible and pettish, where only a few minutes ago she'd had the most blissful experience of her life.

Well, and that was life after all, wasn't it? Blissful experience followed by mundane idiocy. Namely, hers.

"I'm fine, I should go back to my room."

"You can stay for a bit, can't you?" It sounded as though he really did wish she would stay, and she wanted to exclaim at how remarkable it was, that this handsome, strong, smart man was wanting her to stay for a bit longer when all she wanted to do was run off.

"I shouldn't, because if we fall asleep and someone finds us, then we will actually have to get married."

A part of her wanted him to say that it would be fine if that happened, that now that they'd done all this that they should get married. Of course the other part was in vehement disagreement with that, because she'd come to his room without any kind of expectation, and she would never want him to regret this moment.

A long silence during which the two parts warred inside Sophronia's head about what she wanted. No accord had been reached when he finally spoke.

"And I know you don't want that," he said at last. What did he mean? Did he want her to argue with him about it? Tell him she did want it?

She wasn't the one who should be arguing about anything right now. It wasn't as though she went around doing this kind of thing all the time, and knew what to say and do afterward.

Even if you were absolutely and totally in love with the person in question.

Oh no. *Oh no.*

"I have to go," she said hurriedly, pushing herself up off the bed and shaking her night rail back down to her feet. Because if she stayed she might tell him how she felt, and then he would feel obligated to marry her, and then he would eventually resent her, and that was not at all the bargain they'd made.

He stood also, a dazed expression on his face. "Fine, yes. I'll see you tomorrow," he said, his words getting more clipped as he spoke.

"Good night, James," she said, turning to give him one last look.

"Good night, Sophronia," he replied.

What the hell just happened? He'd had the best sex of his life, he'd been in a post-coital bliss when responsibility made him speak, and apparently he'd done the wrong thing.

He thought the men in this situation were the ones who didn't want to discuss such things as contraception and prevention. And what if there was a child? He would want to know, and he would want to do the right thing.

Which he would want to do anyway.

That was the reality of it, wasn't it?

He flopped back on the bed, letting his arms drop to the side, a wash of what might have been heartbreak flooding his senses.

Because he'd never felt like this before—this devastation at the thought of not seeing her after this, of knowing she was out there on her own, in her little cottage that he'd bought for her.

Was it possible he'd gone and fallen in love with her? His pretend betrothed? The one person from whom he didn't wish to escape? The one person who knew that his reckless spirit made it impossible for him to commit to anything—or anyone?

Damn it, he had. He was in love with her, his Sophy, his Sophronia. Who wasn't his at all.

Well, if it were possible to have a more ludicrously appalling situation he didn't know what it would be.

But what he did know was that now that all this had happened, he did not want to let this go. He couldn't let her go.

He would just have to find a way to convince her he meant it.

The next morning he woke up surprisingly alert—probably because he had a woman to persuade he loved her. He'd thought about it for at least an hour, and finally settled on something, something that would hopefully be enough.

Or he'd have to head off into the wilds alone, and he did not want to do that. Not now, not ever again. Not now that he knew what it might be like to be with her.

Thank goodness he'd paid attention when she was speaking—not that he wouldn't have, if he hadn't thought it important, but he hadn't recalled ever paying so much attention to a woman before. When he wasn't in bed with her, at least.

That's how he knew she was different, that she was the one who would intrigue him until they were old and doddering. And until they were old and doddering, he wanted to be with her, to hear her soft moan as he kissed her, feel her curves and skin and watch her descend staircases dressed in fabulous gowns.

"Good morning, everyone." He addressed the room, his gaze alighting—of course—on her. The house was bustling with activity; the villagers were to come gaze on the Greens' magnanimous splendor and perhaps drink a cup of wine before returning home.

She looked startled as he spoke, perhaps because of what they'd done the night before, but also perhaps because he wasn't usually so . . . *sprightly*, if he could call it that, this early in the morning.

He grinned at her, loving how her cheeks pinked up. She had to be thinking about what they had done. If she weren't, then he had seriously misjudged his skill in the bedroom.

"I am planning to go to the vicar's today to view his collection of rare books." He paused. "Sophronia, you needn't accompany me, I think it would be lovely if you stayed here with my mother. I'll return when the party is to occur. Four o'clock, is it?"

Mrs. Green nodded, not looking pleased, but likely too busy to argue or to try to send her daughter along to accompany him.

Sophronia just blinked, and her face froze. He knew she was likely thinking he didn't want to be with her, not after what had happened the night before. He wished he could reassure her, but there was no way to say that without letting his plans for later slip. That is, perhaps there was, but he wasn't confident he could do it.

"Fine, that sounds pleasant." She spoke in a tight tone of voice, and he wanted to laugh at how prickly and goddesslike she was being, only he really didn't think that would do anything for what he wanted from her.

Namely, forever. He wanted forever from her, and he hoped he had thought of the best way to do it.

"Where are you and Jamie planning on settling down?" Mrs. Archer looked hopefully at Sophronia, who wished Jamie—James—Mr. Archer—had not put her in this position. Actually, she was starting to regret she'd been in any kind of position with him, especially the one last night where he was—well, suffice to say she was feeling irked.

Had he planned on that? So it would be easier to say goodbye when this was all over?

It wasn't as though she expected anything, but she had hoped he would seek her out and let her know how he was feeling. Unless he didn't want to let her know what he was feeling, which was why he had gone to Mr. Chandler's house to look at books she knew he had no interest in, for goodness' sake.

And he'd made it impossible for her to go with him, encouraging her instead to stay here with his mother. The mother he was even now duping with her presence, and Sophronia didn't even want to think how the woman would react when she heard Sophronia had died.

And so, though she was angry and hurt and disappointed, she had to admit it wasn't his fault. And she was absolutely and totally in love with him. Still.

Oh, and here she was leaving Mrs. Archer just blinking at her, holding her teacup and regarding Sophronia with a patient look.

"That is something we have to discuss," she replied at last.

Mrs. Archer nodded as though that actually came close to answering her question. Which it did not.

"I was speaking with your lady's maid, Maria she said her name was?" Mrs. Archer didn't wait for a reply. "She is a lovely girl, I was asking her for ideas for—well, never mind that," she said with a knowing look, "but she did say she always hoped to live in a small cottage somewhere, away from the bustle of London." Mrs. Archer sighed. "And I told her that's what we had talked about, and how much I would love to do that. Only if Jamie could find his way to visit, of course, but I would dearly love to have some peace and quiet."

"Yes, that would be lovely." Although the more she thought about it, the more Sophronia wished for some adventure— she'd spent most of her life indoors with her father going through books and reading and visiting. She wanted to go somewhere, just be active and engaged, and not observing.

Perhaps she would find that in her cottage? She didn't hold out much hope for it, but it was definitely better than the poultry she'd anticipated just a few weeks ago. So there was that, at least.

She didn't have any thoughts that hadn't revolved around her fake betrothed and the long endless stretch of loneliness that was to be her future for the next few hours. The house party had dispersed, and Sophronia had seized on the excuse to go up to her room to write some letters.

That she had no one to write to was depressing in and of itself.

She found she was looking forward to the villagers' arrival—she did love seeing people enjoying the holidays, even if the people weren't her.

And wasn't she the most maudlin person ever? She did have a future, thanks to him, that ensured her independence. She wouldn't have to be a poor relation, and next year at this time she would perhaps have found a few friends with whom she could share the spirit of the season.

So when she heard the first arrivals, she descended the staircase from her room, feeling a warmth that was very different from the warmth she'd had in Jamie's arms, in his bed, the night before.

"Welcome, everyone!" Mr. Green seemed to have roused himself, as well, and was greeting the townsfolk at the entrance, a huge smile on his face. Even Mrs. Green looked festive, albeit still disapproving when someone was a bit too cheery.

Sophronia took a cup of wine from a sideboard in the hallway and walked to the large room where the trees were decorated.

She smiled as she heard the audible gasps from the visitors as they caught first sight of them.

And they truly were impressive—all of them were lit, the afternoon sun competing with the glow of the candles for which could be the brightest. There were tables laden with food ringing the edges of the room, and in one corner stood a pianoforte with someone playing a variety of holiday carols.

It gave her a lump in her throat. This, this was truly the spirit of the season, the emotion that she wished she could keep in her heart all year long, even after this magical time was over, because this was what made people joyous. The company of others, simple, quiet beauty, and delightful music. Perhaps accompanied by some food and some wine, always accompanied with the satisfaction of being at peace with oneself.

No matter what would happen from now on, she would be at peace, she promised herself as she gazed around the room. *Merry Christmas, Sophronia*, she whispered softly under her breath.

"Mrs. Green, if you don't mind, I would like to propose a game for the evening." She hadn't gotten a chance to speak with him, not privately, and despite her earlier feelings she was currently vacillating between utter despair that it seemed he didn't care about what they had done the night before and triumph at herself that she had initiated it in the first place. She was not proud of that, but she knew she would return to that earlier, peaceful place eventually.

He, of course, looked the same. Not as though he'd done anything but be solidly, mobile Jamie, although she'd been surprised he'd spent so long at Mr. Chandler's house. He'd arrived halfway through the holiday party and then had left before it was entirely over, returning only when it was time for dinner. She'd caught him glancing at her a few times, a knowing look on his face.

Knowing because he knew what she was like during intimacy? Knowing because he knew the charade they were engaged in? Knowing because that's just who he was?

"Of course, Mr. Archer," Mrs. Green replied. "What do you have in mind?"

They were all in Mrs. Green's capacious sitting room, now comfortable enough with one another after the past weeks that there was none—well, hardly any—of the overstated politeness of new acquaintances. The holiday party had been a success, with the children running around and shooting Christmas crackers at one another, all the food having been consumed, and more than a few bottles of wine, as well.

They'd sung a few carols toward the end, and Sophronia had felt her heart swell even more at hearing the various voices raised together in song.

And there were only a few more nights left. She felt her throat grow tight as she looked around at the company that had been her constant companions for the last few weeks. Soon it would only be her and Maria.

Sophronia and Mrs. Archer were seated together on one sofa, while Miss Green and the viscountess's daughter were to the side in chairs, their heads close together as they whispered. Mr. Green was in the corner, a book on his lap, but his eyes suspiciously closed, while the vicar was standing looking at a bookshelf, his back to the group.

Mrs. Green was also standing, overseeing the disposition of tea.

And Jamie. He was the focus of the room, even for those people who hadn't seen what he looked like without his night-shirt.

"Excellent, Mrs. Green." It was so fast if she had blinked she would have missed it, but he did dart a glance at her. And then returned to looking at the group in general.

"Someone has remarked to me that I win almost all the games." Another quick look in her direction. "And since we are nearly at the end of this delightful visit, I thought I would give others a chance to triumph." He looked at each of them in turn; all of the group, with the exception of Mr. Green, were paying attention to him. "So tonight I would like us to play Dictionary, only I will be the only one supplying the definitions. I cannot vote on the correct one, since I will know it already, and that will give all of you," and this time he definitely looked her way, and what's more, she thought he winked, "a chance to excel."

"That's hardly fair to you, Mr. Archer," Miss Green said in a hesitant voice.

He smiled at her, and Sophronia felt a stab of something—fine, it was jealousy—enter into her ricocheting gallery of emotions.

"On the contrary, it is unfair for me to keep winning all the games." He shrugged. "This way, I get to give all of you a chance."

"That's settled, then," Mrs. Green declared. She spoke to one of the servants who was still in the room, arranging the tea things. "Bring paper and pencils here, and please send Mr. Hotchkiss to the library and retrieve the dictionary."

The servant made some sort of incomprehensible sound of agreement, then scurried out of the room.

Jamie's expression was—sly, mischievous, and nearly delighted. She wondered just what they were in for, since she didn't think this would be a simple game of Dictionary.

"You all know how to play, don't you?" Mrs. Archer shook her head, and Jamie rolled his eyes. "Of course you do, Mother, you and I used to play many years ago."

"Many years ago, Jamie," she said. "Keep in mind I am old, I forget things."

"You're not that old," he said. A brief look of concern crossed his features, and she felt his conflict—to stay a bit longer to please his mother, or to follow his instinct to roam, leaving his mother behind?

She was glad she didn't have to worry about anything like that.

"Since my mother asked, I will remind you all of the rules." He was a born speaker, commanding the room with his handsome presence, his deep, compelling voice and his—well, she had already mentioned his handsomeness, but he was so handsome perhaps it was deserving of a second mention.

"I will choose a word none of you know—if you know, you have to confess it—and then you will all write a definition for the word. We'll vote on which definition is the right one, and whoever gets the most votes for either submitting the best definition or who votes the most often on the correct definition will win."

Miss Green smiled in delight, and Sophronia was struck again by what a pretty girl she was when she wasn't glancing anxiously at her mother. The viscountess's daughter looked bored, but that was probably because it wasn't likely her beauty was going to be the focus of a word. Unless she wrote her own definition.

Sophronia had to stifle a snort at that thought, a brief moment of lightness that showed her that no matter what had happened, no matter what would happen, she was better off than she had been a few weeks ago, when her prospects were poultrylike in nature.

He had done all that for her. And he had done other things for her, too, but she shouldn't be thinking of those things in public, or she knew her expressive face would give her away, and then she and Jamie would be even deeper into the deception.

"The first word is 'agamist.'" Jamie's mouth twisted up in a smirk as he followed with, "Something I no longer am."

"That is not fair, giving hints. The people who know you the best, your mother and Lady Sophronia, will have an undue advantage." Mrs. Green—of course it was Mrs. Green—raised her voice in protest, but nobody else seemed to mind the possible disadvantage.

"Nobody knows that word, correct?" Jamie continued. At everyone's silence, he nodded. "Then you know what to do."

All the people who were playing (Mr. Green had fallen asleep, and was tacitly being allowed to slumber) gathered their pencils and paper and began writing.

Agamist. Sophronia tapped her pencil against her mouth and caught Jamie looking at her, much as he had looked at her the night before. She lowered her gaze to her paper, but not before she felt her face nearly burst into flame.

She thought of something, thankfully something other than an unclothed Jamie, and began to write, smiling as she recalled how zealously her father had attacked the game of Dictionary. As though it were crucially imperative that he devote all of his remarkable brain power to fictitious definitions.

She missed him.

"Is everyone ready?" Jamie didn't wait for everyone to respond, he just began to walk around the room, putting each person's slips of paper into a basket Mrs. Green had thought to provide.

He cleared his throat and began to read. " 'Agamist: a thick fog specific to bodies of fresh water.' " There were a few murmurs around the room as people thought about the word, and its possible definition. Sophronia knew, or at least she thought she knew, that wasn't the correct one, since it was too obvious, the definer using "mist" as the inspiration for the definition.

He continued, reading a few she definitely knew were incorrect. Something about ribbons and books, so likely written by the viscountess's daughter and Mr. Chandler, respectively.

He drew out another piece of paper and cleared his throat. " 'Agamist: A compound of iron and salt.' " That was hers, so that wasn't the right one.

The next one must be it. She tensed, waiting for him to speak. Why it seemed so important she didn't know, just perhaps that she had been wondering where he had gotten to all day, and what he thought about the night before, and if it were possible for them to engage in the activity again before this whole charade was over.

" 'Agamist: A person opposed to the institution of matrimony.' " And her heart stuttered in her chest, because then he met her gaze and raised an eyebrow as though in a challenge, but his mouth was smiling, so she didn't know what to think.

Except that he'd found a word that might mean more than its definition, even though that sounded absolutely odd, and her father would be frowning right now.

But Jamie wasn't frowning. Now he was regarding her with that dashing twinkle in his blue eyes, and now he was grinning at her as though daring her to read into his word.

"Who votes for the first definition?" He didn't take his eyes off her as he spoke.

The viscountess's daughter raised her hand.

Nobody voted for the ribbons and horses definition, and then it was time for hers to be up for voting. "The ore compound definition?"

The Green ladies and the viscountess raised their hands. He still kept his eyes locked on her face, and she felt as though she wanted to squirm in her seat.

"The last definition?"

She met his gaze and raised her chin as she raised her hand. Mr. Chandler and Mrs. Archer raised their hands, as well, and his eyes darted over to them before returning to Sophronia.

"Excellently done. The last definition—the person who is no longer afraid of marriage—is the correct one. Mother, you, Mr. Chandler, and Sophronia each win a point. Sophronia gets three extra points for submitting a definition three people voted on. Well done."

She nodded, wondering if a simple game of Dictionary was meant to be so—so loaded with meaning. That is, it was a game about meaning, but she didn't think it was meant— ha!—to be interpreted as a real life thing. Only what if she was reading more into it than was there? What if his choosing of that word was coincidental?

"Time for the next word," he said, thankfully interrupting her ridiculous musings. They were ridiculous, weren't they? It couldn't be—it couldn't be that—her mind couldn't even go there, it felt so wonderful, and her chest hurt at the thought that it couldn't be, it wasn't, true.

"Gorgonize."

All the players immediately bent to their definitions, the rustling of pencil on paper the only noise in the room. Sophronia tried to think of something, anything, that would be able to fool the room, and eventually settled on something she knew wouldn't fool anybody—well, maybe it would fool the viscountess's daughter, but that didn't count—and waited as the rest of the room finished up, and Jamie collected the papers.

"Gorgonize." He paused and glanced around the room. " 'To have a paralyzing or mesmerizing effect on someone.' "

Her breath caught.

" 'Gorgonize: To turn into stone.' " He grinned, and shot a quick look at the vicar. Of course that was his definition.

" 'Gorgonize. To organize all the things that begin with the letter G.' " He looked at Sophronia with a skeptical look on his face and she returned it with a shrug.

No, she couldn't think of anything right now, not with her head in such a whirl.

He read out the rest of the definitions, and they voted; Sophronia's definition didn't even get the viscountess's daughter's vote, and she had to admit her brain had taken a break since her heart was currently the only organ she seemed to be listening to.

"The definition is to have a paralyzing or mesmerizing effect on someone." Murmurs as everyone exclaimed, and he looked at her, speaking again. "Sophronia gorgonizes me, each and every day."

Oh. She couldn't speak, she could barely breathe. Thankfully, there was no need to since Mrs. Archer made cooing sounds, and even Mrs. Green seemed to smile a tiny bit.

"And now we have another word." A pause as everyone in the room waited, pencils poised above papers. "Appentency."

A silence ensued as everyone got to work on their definitions, their heads lowered to their paper. Sophronia didn't look down immediately, still too caught up in the tumult of what he might be doing to concentrate.

Thank goodness, because then he winked at her, as if to confirm her suspicions, and her heart went from stuttering to fluttering, and she had to take a few deep breaths to keep from bursting out with a question, or several questions, in fact: Are you an agamist now? Does that mean you wish to make this falsehood into a reality? Did you feel the same way I did last night?

Do you love me?

She didn't even bother trying to write a definition, she knew it would result in that "Thingy that does things" definition she'd thought of a previous time he'd managed to fluster and bewilder her.

" 'Appentency: a longing or desire.' " Again, he met her gaze, and there just was no mistaking the look in his eye now. She had just barely stopped herself from leaping up and rushing into his arms when Mrs. Archer spoke.

"Jamie, I feel as though this game is for more than just sport." She nodded significantly to Sophronia. "You are so clever, to woo her like this." She waved her hand in the air. "But don't you know, son, you already have her?"

Jamie looked at her and her breath caught.

"Do I?" he asked softly.

She almost couldn't speak, but she managed to eke out a soft "yes" and a nod of her head.

"Excellent," he replied, his expression looking relieved. And still charming, of course. "And if I may, I would like to break from the game for a moment to osculate my betrothed." A pause. "That means to salute a person on the lips." His eyes met hers. "Namely, to kiss her."

And then he strode toward her as she rose from her chair, guiding her to where the mistletoe hung and kissing her thoroughly on the mouth.

"I love you, Sophronia," he murmured at last.

"I love you, as well, Jamiecakes," she replied. "I am so glad I got my present," she added, a sly, wicked smile on her face, which just made him have to kiss her senseless.

"When will you two be leaving?" Mrs. Archer, as Jamie frequently noted, had her questions reversed; she'd ask them when they were leaving when they'd just arrived, and ask when they'd be returning when they were about to leave.

But now his mother's tone didn't have the same plaintive note from before—now that she and Sophronia's maid Maria had discovered a shared love of small villages and gossip, they'd settled happily into their cottage by the sea, which was close enough to the house he'd found for himself and Sophronia. They still traveled, but the house was an anchor, something he knew he'd be returning to eventually.

He'd found, anyway, that he didn't have the same need to be constantly on the go, now that he had Sophronia. He still enjoyed it, and he liked showing his wife new things, but they were spending more time in England.

And soon, quite soon, in fact, they would be home permanently, since Sophronia was expecting, and neither one of them wanted to deprive Mrs. Archer of seeing her grandchild grow up.

He glanced over to where Sophy sat, his Sophy, the only one who'd been able to soothe him, the one who challenged him, as well, who made him both want to be and to become a better man.

And knew that his reckless taking on of a fake betrothed had been one of the best decisions of his life.

Author's Note

Correct definitions:

Agamist: A person opposed to the institution of matrimony.

Cachinnator: A loud or immoderate laugher.

Otosis: Mishearing; alteration of words caused by an erroneous apprehension of the sound.

Vecordy: Senseless, foolish.

Laetificate: To make joyful, cheer, revive.

Wheeple: To utter a somewhat protracted shrill cry, like the curlew or plover; also, to whistle feebly.

Gyrovague: One of those monks who were in the habit of wandering from monastery to monastery.

Queem: Pleasure, satisfaction. Chiefly in to (a person's) queem: so as to be satisfactory; to a person's liking or satisfaction. To take to queem: to accept.

Peragrate: To travel or pass through (a country, stage, etc.).

Tuant: Cutting, biting, keen, trenchant.

Smicker: To look amorously.

Matutinal: Of, relating to, or occurring in the morning.

Uhtceare: Anxiety experienced just before dawn.

Cunctation: Procrastination; delay.

Aubade: A song or poem greeting the dawn.

Eager for more Dukes Behaving Badly?

**Don't miss the next
full-length novel from
Megan Frampton . . .**

ONE-EYED DUKES
ARE WILD

**Available in print and e-book
December 29, 2015!**

Read on for a sneak peek!

Eager for more Dukes Behaving Badly?

Don't miss the next
full-length novel from
Megan Frampton . . .

ONE-EYED DUKES
ARE WILD

Available in print and e-book
December 29, 2015!

Read on for a sneak peek!

AN EXCERPT FROM
ONE-EYED DUKES ARE WILD

1844
A London ballroom
Too many people, too much noise

Lasham took too big a swallow of his wine, knowing his headache would only be exacerbated by the alcohol, but unwilling to forego the possibility that perhaps, for just a few minutes, his perception would be muffled, blurred a little around the edges.

So that he wouldn't be in a state of constant keen awareness that he was the Duke of Lasham, that he was likely the most important person wherever he happened to be—according to everyone but him—and that he was under almost continuous surveillance.

The ballroom was filled with the best people of Society, all of whom seemed to be far more at ease than he had ever been. Could ever be, in fact. He stood to the side of the dance floor, the whirling fabric of the ladies' gowns like a child's top.

Not that he'd been allowed anything as playful or fun as a top when he was growing up. But he could identify the toy, at least.

"Enjoying yourself, Your Grace?" His hostess, along with two of her daughters, had crept up along his blind side, making him start and slosh his wine onto his gloved hand. Occurrences like this weren't the worst part of having lost an eye—that obviously would be the fact that he only had one eye left—but it was definitely annoying.

"Yes," he said, bowing in their general direction, "thank you, I am."

The three ladies gawked at him as though waiting for him to continue to speak, to display more of his wondrous dukeliness for their delight. As though he was more of an object than a person.

But he couldn't just perform on command, and his hand was damp, and now he would have to go air out his glove before bestowing another dance on some lady he would be obliged to dance with, being the duke, and all. Because if his glove was damp, it might be perceived as, God forbid, *sweaty*, and sweaty-handed dukes might mean that the duke had gotten said sweat because he was enthralled with the person with whom he was dancing, which would lead to expectations, which would lead to expect a question, and Lasham knew he did not want to ever have to ask that question of anybody.

It was bad enough being the object of scrutiny when he was out in public. At home, at least, he was by himself, blissfully so, and taking a duchess would require that he be at home by himself with somebody else, and that somebody would doubtless have ducal expectations of him, as well.

"Excuse me," he said to the silent, gawking ladies. He sketched a quick bow and strode off, trying to look as though he had a destination rather than merely wishing to depart.

"It is my trick, I believe." Margaret leaned forward to gather the cards and swept them to her side of the table, along with the notes and coins that had been tossed in. She glanced to either side of her, noticing the telltale signs of disgruntlement on her companions' faces. She would have to start losing for a bit, then, in order to win more in the end.

Not that she cheated, of course; she was just very, very good at cards, and the people she played with were usually quite bad. Plus she was able to recall just which cards had been played, and that no doubt helped her as she weighed what cards might be coming up next.

It got to be boring, after a while, constantly winning. Though the winnings at the table helped to keep her suitably decked out in the gowns she required in order to keep her place in Society, and also would help some of her other less superficial interests, so she didn't really wish to be losing. Who would wish to lose, anyway?

But sometimes, after she'd won yet another considerable sum, she wished she could be surprised into a loss. To find an opponent who would be worthy of her skill and her attention.

That, it seemed, was not to be. Might never be.

Not that she wasn't grateful to be here at all, she certainly was. The cold truth of it was that she was invited to these events not because she was a good card player, but because she was a scandal, but not too scandalous. So any hostess who invited her would be seen as daring, and she would add color to the festivities, simply because of who she was.

That she was able to support herself and the causes to which she'd dedicated her money was a welcome side effect of her scandalous wake.

"It is your deal, Lady Sophia," Margaret murmured as she passed the cards to her left. The lady took the cards, nodding, and Margaret leaned back in her chair, glancing around the room.

She'd only been back in London for a few months, as soon as she'd found out her parents had departed, and it already seemed as though she hadn't ever left. She'd missed it, even though she'd liked living out in the country, just walking alone for hours at a time and thinking. Just thinking.

Thinking was at more of a premium here, what with all the other things she had to be doing, as well: attending social gatherings such as this one, visiting with her sister, the Duchess of Gage, and her new niece, plotting out how to get her heroine even more in danger with the dangerous hero in her ongoing serialized story, which had just been increased to a weekly publication—another delicious bit to add to her scandalous reputation.

Avoiding her parents.

She felt her jaw clench as she thought about them, how they steadfastly refused to acknowledge her in public since she'd rebelled against their plans for her. As though she would marry someone as loathsome as Lord Collingwood, not that he had any desire to marry her, either. He had just wanted the funds her parents had promised along with her body, and had been dumbfounded when their second—in so many ways—daughter had refused to go along with their plans.

It hurt, even though she should have been accustomed to it by now. And it must bother them, as well, to know that she had returned to Society and had continued to be accepted at parties, and that she was perfectly able to survive on her own. If they thought about it at all, of course.

"Lady Margaret?" Oh, she'd been too engrossed in thinking to realize it was her turn to play. She took a quick survey of her cards, sorted them into their respective suits, and glanced at what had been played. Jack of hearts, two of hearts, and the ten. She had four additional hearts in her hand, as well, which left six other cards. She figured out which ones were missing, then tossed her queen into the pile and took the hand, before laying down a six of diamonds.

It wouldn't do to play too many hearts, she thought to herself ruefully. Not that she had ever given her actual heart. That organ remained intact, not even dented by her close encounter with Lord Collingwood. Her pride, now that stung, but pride would heal; a heart would not.

The play lagged as a footman bearing wine approached the table. Everyone but Margaret took a glass, and then out of the corner of her eye she spotted a large black shape reaching for a glass, as well.

It was a man, of course, a gentleman, since if it were a bear or a mobile rock or something there would have been more screaming and less allowing of the bear/rock to take a refreshment. And as she turned her head to look at him, she felt something inside her stutter to a stop, her breath caught in her throat as she looked.

He looked as though he could have walked right out of the pages of one of her more outrageous serials. He was tall, very tall, taller than all the other gentlemen in the room. And broad, as well, with shoulders that would have strained at the seams of his jacket if the garment in question had been less impeccably cut and less exquisitely molded to his form. His very excellent form.

And that was without even mentioning his face, which was just as excellent. He was clean-shaven, a rarity among the gentlemen in the room, and that meant the sharp planes of his face were clearly displayed. Of course what most people likely noticed was the black patch that covered his left eye, the ribbon tying it on also black, which happened— fortunately—to match the black of his hair and his eyebrows.

As she regarded him, he caught her eye and stiffened, as though he'd recognized her, and didn't want to associate with her, or he hadn't recognized her, but hadn't appreciated her gawking at him.

Either way, she thought with a mental shrug as she returned to the play, he clearly didn't want to have anything to do with her. Pity, since he looked as dangerous as she felt.

"My trick, I believe." Lady Sophia scooped up the coins from the table and Margaret leaned against the back of her chair, only about the seventh most shocking thing she'd done this evening.

The first, of course, had been having the audacity to win at cards despite being a female with a slightly tarnished reputation. The second and third likely had to do with the hat and gown she was wearing—she refused to continue to wear the pale colors of an unmarried woman. The colors didn't suit her, for one thing, and for another, she had no desire to indicate her unmarried status. So instead of insipid ivory, she was wearing blue, and not the wan blue of an early morning sky. This was the fierce, triumphant blue of a cloudless summer at midday.

The numbers leading up to seven likely had to do with declining to dance when asked by gentlemen who thought that because her reputation was tarnished that her behavior would be equally suspect, and taking a second glass of wine. Although she wasn't entirely sure, she imagined that she had likely done things to tick up the number of shocking events that she wasn't even aware of.

And that was why she'd been invited anyway, wasn't it?

It didn't miss her notice that leaning against the back of the chair was just as shocking as refusing a blackguard or a dance. Now if she were a man, she could get away with such behavior. She could lean against chairs, drink as many glasses of wine as she chose, and never have to dance with anyone she didn't wish to. She sighed as the possibility floated above her, like a tantalizing balloon she just couldn't catch.

And then, out of the corner of her eye, she saw another black shape, only this one didn't intrigue her as the pirate had. She knew this man, and she wanted nothing to do with him. Hadn't seen him, in fact, since before her parents had announced she was to be married to him. He hadn't even had the courtesy to come proposing himself, he'd allowed them to tell her what was to be done. Even thinking of it, thinking how close she had come to surrendering her freedom, made her grit her teeth and raise her head as though in challenge.

Although that was incredibly stupid, wasn't it, because then it increased the chances he'd spot her.

"Excuse me," Margaret said, nodding to one of the people watching the card game, "would you mind taking my seat? I find I am need of some air," and she left without waiting for a reply, walking through the crowd quickly in the opposite direction of Lord Collingwood.

Lasham took a sip of his wine with the nondamp hand, squelching the desire to find out just who the lady was who'd met his gaze so—so directly. He wasn't accustomed to that, not at all; either ladies didn't look at him because they were awed by his title or they were frightened by his eye patch. But her—she'd looked at him, and looked at him some more, so he had to avert his own gaze from hers.

He had noticed, however, that while she wasn't as young as most of the debutantes currently giggling in the ballroom, she wasn't old, either. Nor was she beautiful, not in the way of most beauties, but there was something—something *sparkling* about her, as though she'd been dusted in starlight or something like that. A ridiculous thought, and he didn't know where it had come from.

Her hair was a rich, lustrous brown, pulled back from her face with one curl resting coquettishly on her shoulder, which was bare. Her eyes were brown as well, huge, with thick lashes surrounding them. Her mouth was wide and sensuous, if a mouth could be sensuous, and as he regarded her, he'd seen a tiny smile creating a dimple on one cheek. Unlike the usual beauties, she looked utterly, deliciously approachable, which was why he absolutely must not find out who she was or plot to meet her. She looked dangerous, if not in reality, then to his peace of mind.

Lasham continued threading his way through the crowd, nodding to people here and there, keeping his focus away from anyone's eyes so as to avoid conversation. He just wanted, *needed*, a moment away from the party, from the constant scrutiny, from people who kept regarding him as though waiting for him to do something remarkable. Or un-remarkable.

He arrived at a door near where the servants were bustling in and out, turned the handle, and stepped inside, shutting the door softly behind him. He stood in what appeared to be a small library, the streetlamps outside lighting the room enough so he could navigate, even with only one good eye.

He went and leaned against the windowsill, looking out at the street below, the carriages and their patient horses and coachmen waiting for the partygoers to finally decide they were done for the night. At the yellow glow of the streetlamps making the night seem as though it were faintly tinted, at the dark streets with the day's detritus still scattered on the ground.

And he was at last, finally, blissfully alone.

He heard the door open just as he was beginning to gather his resolve to return to the ballroom, to do his duty to the debutantes currently on display, to dance for the next few hours until he could return home and collapse into bed, only to get up and be the responsible duke all over again the next day.

A woman stepped into the room, darting a glance behind her as she shut the door. It was her, of course. The sparkling woman from the card table. That was why she'd been looking at him. He felt the sour taste of it in his throat, the certain feeling that she'd marked him as someone she could manipulate.

"You should go," he found himself saying, even though it was entirely rude and entirely unlike him.

She started, as though she hadn't noticed him, and Lasham felt a twinge of uncertainty.

"I should go?" Her voice held a note of amusement. "I've just arrived, it seems to me that you should be the one to go, since you've been in residence longer. Do allow someone else to have a turn, my lord."

My lord. So she didn't know who he was. Did that please him or annoy him?

"No," he said, and the word, the word he wished he could say to all those people who wanted things from him, wanted him to appear at their events just because he was a duke, slid from his lips as easily as if he'd been saying it his entire life.

"No?" She repeated him, imbuing the word with humor, again, as though that was what she always did. She walked further into the room, her skirts rustling with a soft *sh-sh-sh*. "Then we are here together. Perhaps we should be introduced, although there is no one here to accommodate us." She stepped closer, stopping to rest her hand on the back of one of the sofas. "I am Lady Margaret Sawford." A pause. She tilted her head at him. "And this is where you should offer who you are."

"Oh, yes." Had he ever encountered such an odd woman? But not odd in an unpleasant way. In fact, the way she was looking at him, so directly, so appraisingly, was entirely refreshing. Of course once she knew who he was, that would all change. "*Yes, Your Grace, I will leave immediately.*" Or, worse yet, maybe not—"*No, Your Grace, what will people say if they knew we were alone together? You have compromised me, and now you must do the right thing.*"

"I am the Duke of Lasham. I am pleased to make your acquaintance, Lady Margaret."

She nodded her head, and he saw her smile. "Excellent, Your Grace. Now we are improperly introduced." She gestured to the sofa. "Would you mind if I sat? I promise not to speak, I just want to sit in here a moment."

Lasham couldn't speak himself, he was so taken aback. She—she wasn't here to entrap him, or engage his interest, or anything beyond, apparently, wishing for a moment alone.

He watched as she looked at him for a few more seconds, shrugged, then sat down and leaned her head back, closing her eyes.

"You can sit, as well, if you want." She spoke with her eyes still closed. "If you're not going to leave, which you said you weren't."

"But—" And here Lasham finally found his words. "But if we are discovered, that will put you in a very awkward situation. That is, we being together, it isn't—well, it isn't proper," and didn't he sound like the most stuffy prig in the world, lecturing her on propriety when he'd himself told her no.

She chuckled. "And then what? You will no doubt make all sorts of proper offers, and then I will very improperly say no, and my reputation will be blackened a bit more." She opened her eyes and turned her head to regard him. "It is not the end of the world."

He gaped at her. Not the end of the world? Who was she? Where was the usual response of "Oh, Your Grace, of course, yes, I will leave, or yes, I will marry you, or yes, it will be just as you wish"?

And this woman, this person who'd dared to stare so boldly at him, who'd refused his request, even knowing it came from a duke, had just informed him it would not be the end of the world if they were discovered. That she would not insist on marrying him, or otherwise forcing his hand in any way.

And, contradictorily, that just made him want to know her more.

MEGAN FRAMPTON writes historical romance under her own name and romantic women's fiction under the name Megan Caldwell. She likes the color black, gin, dark-haired heroes, and lots of carbs, just in that order. She lives in Brooklyn, New York, with her husband and son. Visit her website at www.meganframpton.com. She can also be found on Twitter and Facebook, being goofy in various ways.

Discover great authors, exclusive offers, and more at hc.com.

Give in to your Impulses . . .
Continue reading for excerpts from
our newest Avon Impulse books.
Available now wherever e-books are sold.

MONTANA HEARTS:
HER WEEKEND WRANGLER
By Darlene Panzera

I NEED A HERO
A MEN IN UNIFORM NOVELLA
By Codi Gary

BLUE BLOODED
A BENEDICTION NOVEL
By Shelly Bell

BEST WORST MISTAKE
A BRIGHTWATER NOVEL
By Lia Riley

An Excerpt from

MONTANA HEARTS: HER WEEKEND WRANGLER

by Darlene Panzera

Darlene Panzera returns with a sweet
new Western series perfect for fans of
Debbie Macomber's heartwarming romances.

Bree Collins has finally come home to Fox
Creek, Montana, to manage her family's guest
ranch. She knows she can handle any challenges
that come her way, but when the infuriating
Ryan Tanner reappears in her life, Bree suddenly
has doubts about her ability to stay professional—
and away from the handsome cowboy.

Bree stayed a few more minutes to watch them sway in time to the music, then spun around to search for the three CEOs and collided straight into a hard, chiseled chest. A soothing warmth spread over her entire body as she glanced up into Ryan's handsome face and gasped. "You're here."

"I wouldn't miss it."

She leaned to the side and glanced at the three men behind him. "And you brought your *brothers!*"

"Yeah, they're the reason I'm late. They didn't want to come but I knew how much it meant to you, and *why,*" he said, giving her a mischievous grin. "So I had to negotiate a deal to get them here."

Bree smiled because of the way his mouth twitched when he grinned, because of the excitement in his eyes when he looked at her, and because of the way his dark navy blue dress shirt and jeans clung to his splendid physique. *Whoa, girl! Remember to keep it* casual. Recollecting her thoughts, she met his gaze and asked, "What kind of deal?"

Ryan placed a hand on either side of her waist, his touch firm and . . . pleasantly possessive. "I had to trade them my earnings from working your ranch so they can buy a set of new tires for their quad."

He did that for her?

"Which means," he continued, flashing her another pulse-kicking grin, "I'm a little short on money and I'd be willing to be your weekend wrangler for the rest of the summer, if you'll have me."

Stunned, Bree sucked in her breath and stared at him, unable to speak, unable to process exactly what this would mean for her family, unable to think of anything except that Ryan Tanner was absolutely, undeniably, the very, very best! With a little hop, she squealed, unable to hold back her delight, and with her heart taking the lead, she flung her arms around his neck and kissed him.

It was a quick kiss, over before she even realized what she had done, but when Bree pulled back she didn't know who was more surprised, she or Ryan.

His gaze locked with hers for several long, breathless moments, then he cupped her cheek with his hand and drew her back toward him . . . and this time he kissed *her*.

His mouth was warm, tender, and soft against her own and filled with such passion she blocked out every sound around them, every presence, everything except the fact that Ryan Tanner, the guy she'd wanted to dance with since high school, held her in his arms.

An Excerpt from

I NEED A HERO
A Men in Uniform Novella
by Codi Gary

Sergeant Oliver Martinez joined the military to serve his country—not plan parties. But after a run-in with his commanding officer, Oliver is suddenly responsible for an upcoming canine charity event. Worse, he's got to work with the bossiest, sexiest woman he's ever met—who just happens to be the general's daughter. When tempers flare and a scorching kiss turns into so much more, Oliver and Eve will have to decide if this attraction is forever . . . or just for now.

The dog bounded to her, wiggling and licking wherever he could. She held her hand behind her, and Oliver gave her the leash. Once she had it hooked onto Beast's collar, she stood up with a mischievous smile. "I don't know why he gives you so much trouble."

"Oh, I'm sure Best put him up to it," Oliver grumbled.

"Ah, and he gets a kick out of messing with you, huh?"

"That's just because I've let it go until now, but the dude owes me a sofa and chair."

Eve laughed and held the leash out to him. "I wonder if maybe you two just got off on the wrong foot. Perhaps you should open your mind to the possibility that Beast has issues and this is his way of dealing with them."

Oliver took her advice with a healthy dose of skepticism. "What makes you think he has issues?"

"Well, for starters, he came from the animal shelter, so he's got to have some baggage. The question is, was he turned in because he has behavioral problems and his previous owners just couldn't deal? Or were the owners jackasses who just didn't want him anymore?" Her tone was sad as she added, "If he was loved, it's easy to assume that he is confused and misses it."

Oliver studied Eve. Her dreamy, sweet expression tugged at his heart and he wondered who she was thinking about. A loved one she missed? A past lover? A bitter rush of jealousy churned in his stomach. He didn't want to think about another man having even a sliver of Evelyn's affections. Not when he wanted them all to himself.

"How is it you seem to know so much about what he's feeling? Are you an event planner by day and dog psychic by night?" He had been trying to make a joke, but one look at her face told him he'd insulted her.

"I'm just making an observation," she said curtly.

"Hey." He reached out and touched her arm, turning her toward him. "I was just teasing you."

She remained silent, and he took her chin in his hand, tilting her gaze up to meet his. "Why does it always seem like I can never say the right thing to you?"

A small smile played across those bee-stung lips. "Maybe I make you nervous."

Oliver rubbed his thumb across her bottom lip and her sharp, warm breath spread over his skin. "Oh, you definitely make me nervous."

"I do?" Her breathless question stirred his cock to life.

"Yeah, you do. I can't relax around you, not with the way you make me feel," he said.

"How is that?" Her tone was soft, and Oliver dipped his head, his mouth hovering over hers.

"Like I'm standing in the sunshine every time I'm near you," he said.

"Oh."

Oliver didn't give her a chance to escape this time and

covered her mouth with his, groaning as the sweet taste of her overwhelmed him. His hands slid back to cradle the back of her head, sliding his fingers into her hair and loosening her ponytail. A tiny sigh escaped her and he took advantage, slipping his tongue between her parted lips, coming undone when her tongue tangled with his. He felt her hands grip his waist, pulling him tighter against her body and he wanted more. Never had he gotten so caught up in one kiss. And never had he ignored every warning bell for a woman, but with Evelyn, it was like common sense went out the window and was replaced by uncontrolled passion.

Oliver felt something pushing between them and opened his eyes to look down at Beast, who was trying to use his giant head to separate them. Ignoring him, Oliver maneuvered them toward the couch, tumbling Eve down onto the mangled leather.

The kiss broke long enough for Eve's eyes to pop open and she giggled. "Somehow, I never imagined making out on a cloud of couch stuffing."

Oliver grinned down at her. "What can I say? I'm an original."

"You're definitely different," she said.

"Is that a compliment?" His lips found the pulse point behind her ear and he felt her heart race against his mouth.

"I think so."

"You don't sound sure," he murmured against her jaw.

"Probably 'cause I can't think while you're kissing me," she whispered.

His mouth brushed hers. "Want me to stop?"

"God, no."

An Excerpt from

BLUE BLOODED
A Benediction Novel
by Shelly Bell

In the next sexy and suspenseful novel from
Shelly Bell, an investigative reporter and an ex-
military Dom witness a murder outside of the sex
club, Benediction, and uncover a deadly political
conspiracy while trying to clear their names . . .

An Avon Red Impulse Novel

Puffing on his Cuban cigar, the Senator reclined in his chair, a tumbler of scotch on the rocks in front of him. He stared down the two men sitting on the other side of his desk, daring them to repeat the words that had just been uttered.

Sweating profusely, FBI Agent Seymour Fink tugged on his tie, his Adam's apple bobbing above the buttoned collar of his shirt.

For a moment, the Senator considered retrieving his gun from his desk drawer and shooting the agent in the head, but he couldn't risk getting blood or splatters of brain matter on his tuxedo. After all, he had an important dinner to attend in an hour and didn't want to disappoint his wife.

He downed the rest of his drink, then shook the ice in the glass the way he'd like to shake the mobster who was fucking with him. "Tell me what you're going to do to fix the problem," he said calmly, unwilling to allow this minor bump in the road to waylay his plans.

"Do, sir?" Using the sleeve of his suit jacket, Agent Fink wiped the sweat from his brow, cigar smoke circling around his head like a boa constrictor. "I'm not certain we should do—"

"You listen to me, you little prick. There is nothing that

will stand in my way." The Senator hurled his tumbler against the wall above the fireplace, shattering the glass into a million tiny pieces. "Do you understand me? I've got your balls in a vise underneath my blade, so let's try this again. What are you going to do to fix the problem?"

Seymour swallowed convulsively. "No one was supposed to get hurt."

"Don't pull that bullshit now. You knew when I approached you that lives would be lost for the greater good," the Senator said. He handed off his cigar and nodded to the other agent, a bruiser of a man who he'd chosen not only for his twenty years of service to this country, but for his lack of empathy. Agent Richard Evans understood the risks involved in his job, the three bullets he'd taken in the chest a testament to that fact.

Evans pinched the fat cigar between his fingers and in a flash, locked his partner's head under his arm, pinning Fink's hands to the table and singeing the top of one with the foot of the cigar. Fink screamed, his smaller body thrashing wildly as he fruitlessly tried to escape from his partner and the pain he was inflicting.

The acrid scent of burnt flesh overpowered the cigar's sweet one, a smell he would forever more attribute to power.

By the time Evans released him, Fink's skin had turned pasty white, his shirt completely drenched from his sweat. He breathed heavily, nodding. "Consider the problem solved, sir. By this time tomorrow night, Rinaldi will be dead."

The Senator leaned back in his chair and smiled.

God bless the USA.

Touring the dungeon located in the basement of a private mansion, Rachel Dawson ignored the decadent sights and sounds of sex going on all around her and kept her eye on the prize. After working her ass off to gain entrance into Benediction, the prestigious sex club owned by Cole DeMarco, she was finally here.

Although it was early in the evening and most of the upstairs fantasy rooms were still vacant, she'd gotten to play the role of voyeur as she'd observed two different scenes. The "teacher" bending the "schoolgirl" over his desk and smacking her with a ruler had titillated her, but Rachel had remained a removed observer, her body not engaged by the fantasy.

Then she remembered she wasn't at Benediction to fulfill her fantasies or to act as voyeur. She was there to do a story about BDSM and for that, she needed to go to the dungeon.

Unlike the fantasy rooms, the dungeon was packed. In here, the sights, smells, and sounds of passion and pain seduced her senses. The potent scents of leather, musk, and sweat teased her with the promise of sex. Everywhere Rachel looked, people indulged in their kinks without judgment or recrimination.

Her mouth grew dry at the sight of a naked woman suspended from the ceiling by rope and flowing white sheets, twirling as if she was an acrobat in a circus act.

Who had bound that woman? Was *he* here tonight?

An Excerpt from

BEST WORST MISTAKE
A Brightwater Novel
by Lia Riley

Sometimes the worst mistakes
turn out to be the best . . .

Smoke jumper Wilder Kane once reveled in the
rush from putting out dangerous wildfires. But
after a tragic accident, he's cut himself off from the
world, refusing to leave his isolated cabin. When a
headstrong beauty bursts in, Wilder finds himself
craving the fire she ignites in him, but letting
anyone near his darkness would be a mistake.

Quinn unzipped her jacket, pausing halfway. "You don't mind, do you? Seeing as I'm staying, at least for a while."

"No." *Yes.* Because the minute she slid out of that white, puffy coat, her breathtaking body was on full display. Those snug-fitting jeans weren't overtly sexy, but the way the denim contoured to the slight flare of her narrow thighs made him swallow. Hard.

It had been awhile since he'd been in the company of any woman who wasn't a medical professional or intimately involved with his brothers. Also, as much as he didn't want to admit it, he had a type and this forward, strong-looking woman fit it right down to that thick wavy brown hair pulled back at the nape of her long, sexy neck.

Necks were underrated female geography. He loved how they tasted when he kissed them there, how they smelled as he nuzzled.

Equally fascinating was her lush mouth, how the corner remained quirked on one side despite the natural pout, as if in perpetual secret amusement.

This woman was bright, spunky, and happy, despite her father's miserable situation. His heart sank. He had nothing to offer someone like her, not when his whole world had burned to cinder.

He shook himself inwardly, not moving a muscle. No point succumbing to the ugly truth, however true. Maybe he could pretend to be a normal guy for the night. Normal except for the scars, the missing leg, and the fact that he hadn't spoken to a living soul since Sawyer dropped off his groceries six days ago, and was tongue-tied around strangers at the best of times.

Shit.

What would Archer do? His younger brother was good with people, especially the ladies. He'd navigate this situation like a pro.

She gave him a tentative smile, probably because he was staring at her like a loon.

Compliments. Women like compliments.

"Your teeth are real white," Wilder blurted. God damn it, the words hung over them like a comic strip balloon. He wished for a string to grab on to, stuff the idiocy back into his mouth, swallow it down.

"Excuse me?" Her shoulders jerked as her lips clamped, clearly not anticipating the awkward flattery.

At least he hadn't said how much he liked her neck. Yet.